Soldiers in the Mist

by

R. H. Burkett

Soldiers In The Mist

Cover Art by *Debbie Taylor*

The Wild Rose Press, Inc.
PO Box 708
Adams Basin, NY 14410-0708
Visit us at www.thewildrosepress.com

Publishing History
First Fantasy Rose Edition, 2016
Print ISBN 978-1-5092-0775-6
Digital ISBN 978-1-5092-0776-3

Published in the United States of America

I talk to Charlie out loud as if he were sitting across from me drinking morning coffee. Ghosts, however, very rarely (if ever) speak. Not because they can't but because forming words and sentences takes too much energy and time. Speaking out loud is at the bottom of the communication chain in Charlie's dimension.

"So how are we going to write this book if you can't talk aloud to me?" I ask.

Immediately a picture of a shy, handsome young man with chocolate-drop eyes flashes in my mind's eye. Ah...I understand. "A picture is worth a thousand words."

Charlie speaks to me using mental images: a dark, damp graveyard, men gathered around a campfire, cannons flashing. Sometimes he uses emotions instead. Intense feelings of love, hate, guilt, joy, or happiness wash over me until I meld into the character's psyche and we become one.

Automatic writing, however, is Charlie's preferred method of communication and my favorite. I clear my mind, focus on the blank screen before me, and wait for my fingers to spring to life and fly across the keyboard as if they belong to someone else. Which they do. They're Charlie's.

I am conscious of what I type yet not fully aware, much like taking dictation. The experience is so exhilarating that I have to shout, "Go, Charlie, go!" or bust. When I read the manuscript back, I'm in awe. My imagination is great, but no way can I make up what Charlie puts down on the page. I am here to edit, format, and allow my fingers to be Charlie's writing tools.

Dedication

To my mother:
Winnie Watson Burkett
and my grandmother:
Ruth Ely Watson

Acknowledgments

Thank you to all the members of the Northwest Arkansas Writer's Workshop, especially Velda Brotherton. I am a great story teller but Velda made a writer out of me.

Thanks to Linda Apple, Jan Morrill, Paty Stith, and Pamela Foster, my sisters in crime and writing who support and spur me forward.

Thank you to my ex-husband Gregory Weeks, who gave me the newspaper that Sunday morning and set the wheels toward publication in motion.

Whisperings

I am spiritual—some say, psychic. Intuitive is a better word. At numerous psychic fairs I read the Tarot. I run with a pack of free-spirited, fun-loving, liked-minded friends who share the same abilities; however, we don't consider this anything special. Every person is psychic to a degree—some have only developed their awareness more than others. Several of my running buddies "see dead people." Therefore, I wasn't alarmed when they informed me one afternoon that a Confederate soldier was standing outside my living room window.

I live close to the Pea Ridge, Arkansas where a major Civil War battle took place. Rebel soldiers probably camped in my backyard, so this discovery wasn't a major surprise.

Wonder if he knows he's dead?

"Yes, he does."

I stare at my friend, bemused. I hadn't voiced the question out loud.

Wonder what his name is?

"His first name is Charles. Having trouble with his last name. Something like Eli."

She has my full attention now—I hadn't spoken this question, either.

"Could it be Ely?" I ask.

"Yeah. That's it. Ely."

Chill bumps cover me like a blanket, and I shiver. Impossible. Ely is my grandmother's maiden name, and she had a brother named Charles. My friend knows nothing of my family tree. Could this soldier be a distant relative?

No sooner had this thought crossed my mind when my friend exclaims, "Oh my God.

He's on his knees, crying." She looks at me, puzzled.

I tell her of the family connection. She smiles. "His tears are from joy and relief. He's waited for you to move here for a long time."

A mystical game of connect-the-dots begins. Charlie's appearance is Dot #1.

Charlie haunts me in more ways than one. Why does he wait for me? Is he really a blood relative?

My brother's library contains books that are passed down through the generations of family members. I search the shelves, turning page after page in worn, tattered editions until I find one that stops me cold. On the inside cover, in his own handwriting, is the inscription, "This book is the property of Charles Ely." Dot #2.

My brother and I put our heads together, check birthdates, and do the math. The time line is correct. Charlie was nineteen during the time of the Civil War. Dot #3.

I research Civil War names on the Internet. There is a Charles Ely listed. Dot #4.

Unlike my friends, who literally see ghosts, I feel their presence more. That's not to say, however, that on certain occasions, a shadowy figure hasn't materialized before me. I sit on my porch swing and think of

Charlie. What does he want from me?

A shimmering, much like heat waves rising from the pavement, stirs the misty twilight, and Charlie stands before me. "Tell my story. You must swear."

The game ends. The journey begins.

While I fancy myself intuitive, I have to admit communicating with ghosts on a regular basis was a new adventure for me. In writing this book, there were many strange and bizarre happenings. I thought it would be fun and interesting to share these with you.

Sprinkled though out the chapters are actual conversations and experiences that occurred while working with Charlie and his comrades called, "Whisperings."

Believe these encounters or not.

Please try to keep an open mind, however; a closed one misses so much.

~R. H. Burkett

Prologue

He came to me at twilight.

Twilight—that magical time of day when the barrier between dimensions melt and souls time-travel with ease.

He stepped forward from the mist.

At first I questioned the sanity of my vision. But the good-looking soldier stood rock-solid in defiance of my wavering mind. Dressed in Confederate gray, his deep brown eyes held me spellbound, and I listened to his words in silent wonder.

"My name is Charles Ely, your cousin. I've waited for you for over one hundred and fifty years."

One by one, more soldiers materialized from the haze: a red-headed, freckled man with laughing eyes; a handsome man with shoulders wide as a mountain; even a teenage girl; all in all, thirty-five men with horses.

"We're angry," Charlie said. "Our blood is in this land. No one knows. No one cares. We are lost. Doomed to wander through time without hope. Only you can release us. You must write our story. It is your destiny as sure as war was ours. You must promise."

The mist swirled.

I stood alone.

And so it began.

Charlie returned every night to give his story of the

Confederate Horse Soldiers of Unit 547.

Three men. Three promises—two were broken; one should have been. Thirty-five souls are trapped for eternity because of those promises. These souls wait and search for the fourth promise that will set them free...

Chapter 1

Charlie's Story

Thud! Charlie jumped at the sound.

Thud! Another shovel of dirt hit the wooden coffin.

Thud! Sickening. Final.

He feared the sound would haunt him the rest of his life. The preacher droned on, "Ashes to ashes, dust to dust." Over-used words that held little meaning and gave no comfort.

Thud! The smell of damp, upturned earth filled his nostrils, and little boy tears stung his eyes.

Inside the hold of his mother's grasp, his hand sweated, and the urge to pull away tempted him. Yet he stood firm. He lifted his gaze from the dark hole to her face, drawn and pale, lips pressed together in a tight line.

Thud! A chill ran up his spine. Where were her tears? She cried none, not from the time she'd found Pa lying face down in the dirt of the cornfield to now, being covered with soil lying face up in a pine box. Like she expected it. A shudder touched his shoulder. Maybe she had. Mother had a strange way of knowing things were going to happen before they did. Pa called it *The Shine*.

He stole a glance at the people standing silent around the burial site. Only five, including the preacher who didn't count. He had to be there. No tears gathered in the corners of their eyes either. Pa worked hard, held to the Golden Rule, and only a handful of people gathered out of respect for him? A man's life should mean more. A week, a month, a year would pass and all trace of his life would be gone. Would anyone remember? Surely to God, Mother would. Surely to God, one day she would weep tears of sorrow. But not today. Today his tears were the only ones that fell and hit the coffin's lid.

Thud.

Still holding his hand, she walked away, ramrod straight. Not once did she glance back. He couldn't help but look. Pa was under that dirt. Didn't anyone care? Tears clouded his sight, and he stumbled as she pulled him along. He climbed onto the wagon seat beside her and wiped his snotty nose on his sleeve. The sound of her deep sigh broke the silence.

"It's just you and me, Charlie. You're the man of the house now and must be strong. I know it isn't right, but life is hard and seldom fair. You're all I have. Promise me you'll never leave, Charlie."

What was he to do? He was only nine, Pa was dead, and Mother needed him. He lifted his chin and did the only thing he could do.

"I won't, Mother. I promise. I'll never leave you alone."

Charlie walked the creek bed searching for a smooth rock and kept his gaze low.

Held by the promise he'd made when he was nine-years-old, he didn't want this friends to see the uncertainty in his eyes. Would they think he was being foolish and acting like a child?

"Did you tell your ma yet?"

Charlie threw the rock side-armed. Three skips. He shook his head. "No, not yet."

"Aw, for Pete's sakes, Charlie. Grow a backbone. We're leaving in a few days. You're running out of time."

He picked up another rock and resisted the urge to throw it at his best friend. James was headstrong and reckless and had a knack of pushing their friendship too far. Charlie finally asked, "How'd your ma and pa take the news?"

"Pa just shook his head and said 'a man's gotta do what a man's gotta do.' Ma was madder than a wet hen. First she forbid me from going. When that didn't work, she started crying." He picked up a pebble and weighed it in his hand. "She always makes mountains out of mole hills."

A loud guffaw sounded behind them. "Riding off to join the war is a pretty big mole hill, if'n you ask me."

"Shut up, Tom. Nobody did."

Charlie winced. Tom always put himself in the other person's shoes, which made him a natural-born peacemaker. But sometimes James took advantage of his easy going nature and spoke too rough. "What did your pa say, Tom?"

Busy trying to bait his hook, Tom's brow creased. Once the wiggling worm was hooked securely, he pushed his cap back off his head and cast his line into the murky water. Straw colored hair escaped and flopped into his eyes. "Aw, you know Pa. He don't ever say too much. He kinda got a sad look in his eye but never said yea or nay. James is right, Charlie. You gotta tell your ma. What'cha waitin' on? Pa said he'd take care of your stock and ride out and check on your place."

James threw his stone and hit a turtle sunning itself on a moss covered log. The hard shelled critter slid off into the floating algae with a dull plop, and the scent of green pond scum drifted through the air.

"Yeah, Charlie. What's the hold up? My folks said your ma was welcome to move into town and stay with them at the boarding house until we come back. It ain't like you're abandoning her. She makes decent money teaching school. Everyone in town says she's the best teacher they ever had, and they ain't never gonna fire her. She won't lack for nothing."

He studied the stone in his hand. Easy for them to talk. They hadn't made a promise. "You don't understand."

James's sarcastic snort echoed through the trees. "Oh...the promise." He cut Tom a look and rolled his eyes. "Here we go again."

Tom grinned, but said nothing.

"Charlie, the three of us have been best friends since Heck was a pup," James said. "We know your ma. Next to mine, she's the strongest woman I know. Sure, you made her a promise. What kid wouldn't in a situation like that? But it was over ten years ago. No one should hold you to a vow made in the shadow of death, especially her. If you ask me she had a lot of nerve asking it of you."

The rock flew from Charlie's hand and struck James on the forehead.

"Hey! What the hell—"

Charlie was on him like a duck on a June bug,

striking him low at the knees. James went down like Goliath and hit the stone ground with a hard smack. The wind left his lungs. Not caring that his friend was powerless to defend himself, Charlie pummeled away.

"You arrogant little piss ant! Take that back!"

Tom dropped his pole and scurried toward them, slipping and sliding on the slick rocks. He grabbed Charlie's shirt collar and hauled him off James, holding him like a mad dog on a leash. James struggled to his feet. Blood trickled down the side of his face into his mouth. He spat and moved toward Charlie with clenched fists.

"Stop it! The both of yas! Christ sakes, you're acting like a couple of mangy tomcats. We're blood brothers, remember? Jimboy, you had no right saying that about his ma. You weren't there. It weren't your daddy that died. Apologize. And Charlie? Even though what James said was worded wrong, there's still a grain of truth in it. Your mama does take advantage of that promise and leads you around like a prized steer. To be fair, I don't think she knows what she's doing. She controls your life. You're nineteen and a man. Don't ya get tired of it?"

The words took the fight out of him, and Tom's voice of reason hit a nerve at the same time. Yes, he got tired of it. Mother dictated his every move, and he no more felt like a man than the rock he'd cracked James's skull with.

"I'm sorry, James. You okay?"

"Oh, sure." A silly grin spread across his face. "Good thing I'm hard headed, ain't it?

I'm sorry too, Charlie. Tom spoke true. I didn't have the right."

Charlie reached over and gave Tom a playful punch on the shoulder. "Yeah, Tommy's correct about a lot of things. I'll tell Mother at breakfast tomorrow."

"Whew!" Tom exclaimed. "Glad that's settled. Now, can I go fish?"

Whisperings

I talk to Charlie out loud as if he were sitting across from me drinking morning coffee. Ghosts, however, very rarely (if ever) speak. Not because they can't but because forming words and sentences takes too much energy and time. Speaking out loud is at the bottom of the communication chain in Charlie's dimension.

"So how are we going to write this book if you can't talk aloud to me?" I ask.

Immediately a picture of a shy, handsome young man with chocolate-drop eyes flashes in my mind's eye. Ah…I understand. "A picture is worth a thousand words."

Charlie speaks to me using mental images: a dark, damp graveyard, men gathered around a campfire, cannons flashing. Sometimes he uses emotions instead. Intense feelings of love, hate, guilt, joy, or happiness wash over me until I meld into the character's psyche and we become one.

Automatic writing, however, is Charlie's preferred method of communication and my favorite. I clear my mind, focus on the blank screen before me, and wait for my fingers to spring to life and fly across the keyboard as if they belong to someone else. Which they do. They're Charlie's.

I am conscious of what I type yet not fully aware, much like taking dictation. The experience is so exhilarating that I have to shout, "Go, Charlie, go!" or bust.

When I read the manuscript back, I'm in awe. My imagination is great, but no way can I make up what Charlie puts down on the page. I am here to edit, format, and allow my fingers to be Charlie's writing tools.

Gives a whole new meaning to the term "ghost writer."

~*R. H. Burkett*

Chapter 2

Charlie balanced the load of firewood in his arms and nudged the door open with the tip of his boot. The strong smell of coffee greeted him, and he took in a deep breath, savoring it. "Here's more wood, Mother."

"Thank you, Charlie, you're a good boy. Breakfast will be ready shortly."

A twinge of irritation nipped at him. Boy. Why did she always call him boy?

Unable to resist the coffee's aroma, he poured a cup and sat at the table. Breakfast was his favorite time of day. He liked the way the rising sun poked its head through the kitchen window and cast golden rays across the floor and against the walls, giving the room a cozy, cheery feeling. The woodsy smell of hickory bacon drifted throughout the small cabin and his mouth watered.

Deep in thought, he traced the carved lines etched into the crude kitchen table. A small grin tugged at the corners of his mouth. Many nights he had sat at that table and studied by the glow of the lantern's light while Mother knitted and rocked by the fire. The smile faded. Where would he find words and the courage to tell her he was leaving? And why were childhood memories jumping to mind to sabotage his decision?

"Remember how you taught me sums at this table? Never thought I'd get the hang of them, but you wouldn't let me quit. Then one day it all made sense."

A plate of warm biscuits smeared with honey appeared before him. She patted his shoulder and smiled. "We have a lot of good memories, thanks to this ol' wooden table."

His teeth sank into the flakey crust, and honey dripped from the corners of his mouth. He wiped his lips with his thumb, then licked the sticky, golden ooze off. The sizzle of potatoes she sliced into bacon grease made him glance at the stove, and he watched her with a heavy heart. Her hair flowed free this morning, running down her back in charcoal ringlets. Usually she wore it braided in a single strand, but he preferred it loose. Freed from their tight weave, locks curled around her neck and softened her features, making her look younger.

He frowned into his cup and tried to remember when her face hadn't been lined, and her hair wasn't the color of smoke. Age was the only thing that contradicted her apathy toward Pa's death.

He shuddered at the memory of that awful day when she stood solid as an oak. Not once had she shown sadness or wallowed in self-pity. He knew people respected her. Often he overheard them say, "Clara Ely may be tiny in stature, but she's a tower of strength in every other way." Only he knew how much she leaned on him. Guilt pricked his heart.

The bread turned to dough and stuck to the roof of his mouth. He swallowed hard several times. He was fixin' to turn her world up-side-down, and it made him sick to his stomach. But was it fair to forfeit his whole life to her? Maybe Tom had been right. Perhaps she didn't realize the depth of her dependence on him. If only he could make her understand.

He took a deep breath. "Mother, I talked with James yesterday."

"That's nice, son. He's a fine boy. His folks were such a help to me after your father passed. Wish I had some onion to throw into this mix."

Her indifference and nonchalant tone irked him. *Stop stirring the potatoes and listen!*

"James isn't a boy, Mother. And neither am I."

"What is that supposed to mean?"

Now that he had her full attention his bravery wavered. Sweat beaded on his forehead, and he struggled to collect his wits again. "James joined the war. He's leaving for Richmond in a few days."

Her back stiffened. "You know how I feel about this war talk. It upsets me, and I'll have none of it."

He swallowed hard. "Yes, ma'am. But…"

"No buts, Charles!"

The small lump in his throat grew to walnut size. She never called him by his Christian name unless she was angry…or scared. "Mother, we have to talk about it."

She slammed the spoon on the stovetop and wheeled. With short, direct steps she marched to the table and grabbed a chair but didn't sit down. Instead, she learned hard on it and clutched the slatted back so tight her knuckles turned white. The heat from her stare seared his soul, and he cringed.

"Why? Why must we talk about it, Charlie?"

"Mother."

"Don't dare tell me you're going, too."

He said nothing.

"No. I forbid it."

Forbid? Blood roared in his ears. "You can't stop me, Mother. I'm nineteen and grown."

"Charlie, I beg you, don't. If you go, you'll not return."

"You don't know that for sure."

The look on her face told him different, and his breath caught. *The Shine.* Had she foreseen his death just as she had Pa's? She told him about the vision that came disguised as a dream. How she seen Pa collapse in the field. If there had been any doubt, the owl dispelled it when the night bird called out its warning days before. Mother considered the animal a winged prophet that foretold death.

Uncertainty and a pinch of fear crept into his resolve and caused his tone to turn flippant. "Heard the owl lately? Had a vision?"

Hurt replaced the worry in her eyes. He shouldn't have said that.

"Watch your mouth, Charlie. Don't make fun of the things you know nothing about. I've never asked you to believe in the sight, only that you keep an open mind. I have a mother's heart. It knows you won't return."

"I'm going. I have to."

He thought he knew her every side. She seldom raised her voice to him in anger. Never had she struck him, but the fury that burned in her eyes made him wonder. He pushed back from the table and braced for the blow.

Her chair suffered the attack. She flung it from her, and it took on a life of its own.

Skidding across the floor, the wood screamed as it hit the iron stove. Fractured wooden limbs littered the floor. Great grandmother's teapot rattled in protest from its seat of honor on the only shelf that graced the kitchen walls.

Shocked, he jumped and his chair overturned. He gaped at the busted furniture then at her. Never had he seen her so angry. Who was this woman standing before him? Face ashen. Eyes shooting hazel bullets.

His head reeled. The room spun. What had he done? It wasn't supposed to be this way. Her uncharacteristic rage shook him to his core. He closed his eyes and took a calming breath. "Mother, the North wants to control us and free our slaves. It's my duty to fight."

Her scornful laugh bounced off the kitchen walls. "Slaves? You see any slaves on this place, Charlie? For that matter, have you seen slaves anywhere in this town? Son, this war isn't about slavery. That's just a handy excuse. It's a means to rile up young men's emotions. Judging from the way you're acting, it worked. It's a way to justify the killing. Every war ever fought or will be fought is only about two things, power and greed. I raised you to think for yourself. You've more sense than this. Give this more time. More thought. You're only nineteen and just a—"

"Just a what? A boy?"

"Don't put words in my mouth, Charlie."

"But that's what you were going to say, wasn't it? That's all I am to you, isn't it? And if I stay here that's all I'll ever be. You're smothering me, Mother. That's why I have to go. I have to prove to everyone, including myself, that I'm more than a snot-nosed kid tied to his mother's apron strings."

He watched tears spring to her eyes and drown the

flames shooting from them.

"Is that what you think? Years don't make a man, Charlie. Some boys become men at nine years of age while others live a lifetime and never grow up. I'm sorry for holding on to you so tight, but I knew the day would come when you would go. I wanted to delay it as long as possible. Young men have to sow their oats, but war isn't the place to begin. Perhaps that's selfish of me. Maybe I made a mistake not to call you a man, but that's a mother's irony. No matter how old our children become, we always consider them our babies."

The smell of burning potatoes made her turn from him and return to the stove. Her shoulders slumped and like her broken chair, his heart shattered into pieces. This was the first time he'd ever defied her.

"When are you going?"

"In a few days. I'm moving you into town tomorrow. James said his folks want you to live at their boarding house. His mother doesn't want him to go either. She said it would be a comfort if you stayed with her. You'll be closer to school, and it'll be safer than staying here by yourself."

"Guess I was wrong, again. Looks like you *have* given this some thought."

The coldness of her voice settled on his shoulders like a damp fog. Without a word he swept the chair limbs from the floor and placed them in the firebox by the stove. The room closed in around him. He grabbed the water bucket and started out the door. The sound of her tears stopped him. In disbelief he turned and stared. She hadn't shed one tear in ten years over Pa's death, but she wept today because of him. His words had burned and scarred. The feeling grabbed his heart and squeezed.

"Mother, I swear to you. Everything will be fine, and I will come back. I prom..." No! Wouldn't promise. Not ever again.

She said nothing. Too many words had been said as it was. His mind was made up, and nothing he could say would change hers.

He continued to stare.

She stood defeated.

Old and alone.

Chapter 3

A wet, woolen blanket of silence hung between them, and Charlie would've given anything to take back some of the words he'd spoken. He hadn't understood. If only she'd shared her feelings before now. His lips flattened into a hard line. The quarrel wasn't all her fault. He should've told her how he felt long before now, too.

She walked with stiff steps from the cabin to the wagon and refused to take his arm when he tried to help her onto the hard seat. He sighed and returned to the wagon bed to check the ropes that held her belongings in place. If Grandmother's teapot got broken, he would never forgive himself. Satisfied everything was secure, he stepped up into the wagon, gathered the reins, clicked to the team, and watched them strain into the harness.

The road was rough and uneven, and she grabbed the side rails to steady herself as the spring seat bucked and pitched. She turned and gave their home a long winsome look, as if seeing it for the last time. The pain in her face stabbed his heart deeper than any blade, yet it aggravated him as well. Wasn't like she was leaving for good.

"Mother, this move is only temporary. The war won't last long. We'll be back home before you know it."

He glanced at her from the corner of his eye and caught her smug expression as if she knew something he didn't. Still, no words passed between them. Nothing—not even war—could be worse than this stillness. His head pounded, and he withdrew into himself. If this was how she wanted it, so be it. The ride into town would be a long one.

Butcher Knife Creek snaked its watery skin around trees and rocks and followed alongside of them with a lazy, tranquil current. A tanned blur of a doe and her fawn shot across the trail. He followed the deer's white tail as it disappeared into the thick foliage and uttered a silent prayer that the mother and baby were upwind from the cougars.

Pumas roamed the holler day and night indifferent to the humans that spotted them. Their daring behavior became the talk of the town which prompted the editor of the newspaper, Ruth Watson, to write a commentary about how the creek and holler were home to bold, golden-skinned cats that feared neither man nor beast. She suggested the town be named *Cougar Hollow, Virginia* and everyone agreed. Her daughter, Winnie, painted a large white sign with a sleek, panther cat stretched out below the name. It marked the beginning of Main Street, and Charlie heaved a sigh of relief as he drove past it. Thank God they were here. Another mile of Mother's self-inflected anguish would have his nerves in such a tight knot he'd be walking like he had a cob up his butt.

James waited for them on the steps of the boarding house and helped Charlie unload the wagon. "Rough trip?" he asked.

"You could say that. Heard any news about when

we move out?"

"Not yet. Ya want to mosey on down the street? Town's like a beehive today."

"Yeah, that sounds good. I need to get my mind off Mother."

"She'll come around, Charlie. Ma and her are drinking tea and talking it out as we speak. We just took them by surprise, that's all."

Charlie shook his head. "Hope you're right. I can't take much more of Mother not talking to me. We've never argued. Her silence is deafening. I'd rather she scream and yell."

"Naw, you wouldn't." James grinned. "Trust me, I know. Let's get a big ol' sour pickle at Goldstein's and see if anyone's heard any news."

Charlie laughed, and they joined the group of men milling about in Goldstein's Dry Goods Store. Cougar Hollow didn't have a saloon, and Goldstein's became the unofficial meeting place by default. Not that the Hollow was dry. On the contrary, homemade corn mash and moonshine could be found in many homes. The demon drink just wasn't sold on Main Street.

The air in the store was charged with excitement as husbands, fathers, and sons spit tobacco, played checkers, and talked about the war. Charlie watched as James fished a fat dill from the barrel, then edged his way to the back of the room to join him. Together they listened to the conversations with growing anticipation. A feeling of apprehension mingled with the scent of leather and coffee and circled the room. Charlie shifted his weight from one foot to the other and tried to shake his uneasiness. It was the waiting, that's all. He eyed the room. Everyone was leaving loved ones behind. No one knew what to expect and speculation of where they were going was as varied as the canned goods that stocked the shelves and counters. He sighed, ran his sweating palms down his pants legs, and wished for some sort of news to come quickly. Word came at suppertime.

He searched for Mother.

She sat in the rocking chair on the back porch of the boarding house. He hesitated and drank in every detail of the moment, pressing it like a dried flower between the pages of his memory book. Weeping willows surrounded the veranda and bowed in wispy sorrow to the earth while the lonely call of the whippoorwill echoed off the hills. The setting sun caught and held her in the magic of its gold and orange aura. She once told him never to judge others as angels sometimes walked the earth in human form. He hadn't believed her, until now. Never would he forget how peaceful and beautiful she looked, and he thanked God for the picture He graced him with in that brief wrinkle in time.

He knelt beside her and stopped the rocker's creaky sing-song melody. He chewed his lip. Time had run out and he couldn't leave knowing the chair-throwing incident would be their last words to one another. Somehow he had to find a way to reach her.

"Mother? Today is Sunday. Monday we leave. Mother, please. I'm sorry. I didn't understand, and I never intended to hurt you. Mother? Did you hear me?"

A muscle quivered in her jaw. She reached out, took his hand, and patted it. A sad smile as faint as a hummingbird's wing flitted across her face. "Yes, Charlie. I heard. I didn't understand either."

And just like that, the tension between them melted. What caused the change? He didn't know. Maybe she didn't want anger to be their parting gift to one another either. No matter. Relief flowed through his veins like warm milk and calmed his ragged nerves.

"Charlie, walk with me. I've something to show you."

Curiosity shot through him, and she laughed. "Oh, you should see your face. It reminds me of how you looked on Christmas mornings when you were little. Seems like no matter how old a man gets, he never gets tired of surprises."

Warmth replaced his inquisitiveness. A man. She called him a man.

Twilight fell, and the dusty street faded into shadow. Merchants lit lanterns hung on store fronts and posts. Their soft glow softened the town's sharp edges and added to the twinkling of the fireflies that zipped past them. They walked in comfortable silence until she stopped in front of the livery stable and called out, "Harvey? It's Clara Ely."

Harvey Carpenter limped out of the stable leading a sleek, long-legged sorrel gelding. He handed the lead rope to Charlie.

"His name is Red. Part Thoroughbred. Eight-year-old. Runs like the wind. Jumps like a deer."

Instinctively Charlie took the lead, but all conscience thought froze. What was Harvey doing? A gentle touch on his arm made him glance away for the horse's burnt copper coat and onto his mother's teary smile.

"He's yours, Charlie. I won't have my son on foot in this war. You'll be safer on horseback. I asked Mr.

Carpenter to find a strong, fast horse for you." She winked at Harvey. "You did an excellent job. He's magnificent."

This wasn't real. It was a dream. Trancelike he reached out and ran his hands over the horse's slick shoulders, certain his touch would dissolve the vision. The strength that rippled beneath the mount's mahogany skin felt real enough. With easy fingers he traced the snippet of pearl that trickled from the animal's flat forehead to a pool of white at his muzzle. Proud, intelligent eyes blinked at him.

"Mother? How? We ain't got no money."

"Charlie. Such language. I taught you better."

He smiled. Always the school teacher.

"Harvey and I made a deal, that's all. Mothers can be very resourceful when necessary."

He chuckled, convinced she could move heaven and earth if need be. Her words broke into his thoughts.

"There's more. On the saddle."

Looped around the saddle horn hung a brown leather gun belt and holster. His hands shook when he pulled the shiny revolver from its leather pouch.

"It was your father's." Her voice broke. "I was saving it for your birthday, but you have need of it now."

Tears nipped at his eyelids, and he buried his face in Red's toffee-colored mane to hide them. He never knew Pa owned a pistol. The memory of that day washed over him. The sharp wind bit his face, his head throbbed from fighting tears, and his hand sweated inside Mother's firm grip. He feared time would erase Pa from his mind, and he longed for anything that would hold his memory, but there was nothing. This gift was a lifeline back to him. Overwhelmed, he hugged the revolver to his chest and struggled to speak.

"Mother...the pistol...Red—it's too much. You made quite a bargain."

Behind them Harvey cleared his throat and fumbled for words. "I—um—I got this here pocket watch that belonged to my daddy. He got it from his daddy. My son, Tom, is leaving too." He dipped his head, and a blush crept up his leathered neck. "Reckon ya know that seeing how the two of yas is thicker than tree sap. Ya think he might want it? I mean, he might need to know the time riding on the trail. Savvy?"

Charlie smiled. Harvey Carpenter was a simple, proud man of few words, and he knew how difficult it must have been for the old horse trader to ask his opinion. The bowlegged, little man didn't have much except his reputation as an experienced horseman, and his son. Now, Tom was leaving and just like Pa's pistol, the watch would be Harvey's link to him.

"Yes, sir. I understand completely. I know Tom would be honored to carry such a fine timepiece."

A faint smile crossed the old man's face. "I best be getting on with the feeding. I'll put the horse back in his stall for ya." He tipped his hat. "Nite, Mrs. Ely."

Charlie took her hand and squeezed it with silent affection. His heart fluttered. "Mother? Where is your wedding band? I don't feel it."

"Oh? Dear me. I must have left it in the kitchen when I helped Alice wash the supper dishes. How forgetful. I guess it was the excitement of the evening."

Her mock surprise didn't fool him. The gold band was the only thing of Pa's she had left, and she never took it off. Everything made sense now. She traded the ring for Red. He opened his mouth to protest, but stopped. She sacrificed the ring out of love. To keep him safe. Maybe she thought a fast, brave horse could save his life. Bring him back to her. True, it was a long shot, but it was the only thing she could do, and to betray her secret would do more harm than good. Love poured into his heart until the emotion ran over and pushed tears from his eyes. He wiped them on his sleeve and made a silent vow that one day the ring would return to her.

His arm encircled her and he pulled her to his side. She leaned into his hard strength. Arm-in-arm they walked into the blissful silence of the evening.

He wondered if this would be the last they would ever spend together.

Chapter 4

Clara stood at the bedroom window and watched the sunrise splash the sky with streaks of pastel yellow and blue. Crows winged their way across the newborn horizon and cried greetings to the dawn. The night denied her sleep, and Monday morning came too soon. How dare this day be so bright when her heart bled darkness. Mother Nature had played a cruel trick.

Her eyes lost focus. She traveled to a smoky, frosty morning in a time yet to come. Soldiers. Gray-clothed men going about their morning duties and routines.

Gunshots.

Screams.

Death.

She shook free from the trance. Wasn't the first time the vision had come to her, but this time it was different. This time Charlie's face wasn't there. Why? Red? Dare she believe that she'd changed the outcome by providing Charlie with an advantage? After all, Red was only a horse. But what an animal. She'd prayed God would provide a wonderful mount, but not in her wildest dreams did she imagine the grandeur of Red. He was hope with four legs and a tail. Hope that Charlie would cheat death and come back to her. The wedding ring had been a small price to pay. A ring could be replaced but not her child.

She sat on the edge of the bed, braided her hair into

a belt of woven silver and charcoal, and took a deep breath.

It was time.

Alice Johnson stood by her shoulder in the early morning light. Silent and tight. "Damn fool men." Alice spat. "They act like war is some glorious thing."

"Nothing is good about war. Nothing is grand about your babies dying in some God-forsaken place, alone and scared. War is a lot of things, but no matter how noble the cause, it is never grand. I tried explaining that to Charlie, but he refused to listen."

"Don't punish yourself for it, Clara. I failed as well. In fact, I'd wager every mother here lost that battle. At first I forbid Jimmie from going, then I begged, finally I cried. There was nothing I could do or say to stop him. It was the first time I was unable to persuade him to my will. He just stood there. So sure of himself. Ever so much the man. He picked a fine time to grow up. Youth. They think they know it all."

Clara said nothing and watched the scene playing out before her with an aching heart.

The street hummed with activity. Fathers. Sons. Brothers. All surrounded by their loved ones, fighting tears and time, knowing they could stop neither. The older men beamed with pride at the younger ones. But it was a different story with the mothers. Some stood together, wringing hands and wiping tears. Some cradled their son's face with trembling hands, forever etching the memory of their babe's image in their hearts. Some wept openly, unashamed. Others stood in agonized silence. Stunned and empty.

Horses sensed the sorrow and stamped hooves and pawed the ground in protest. Dust swirled and circled the crowd. Snorting and shaking their heads, they signaled their impatience and desire to run. The breath from their nostrils circled the crowd and looked like dragon smoke floating though the frosty air.

One-by-one men began to form the column that would take them away from their families and toward an unknown future. Charlie walked to her. Her heart skipped a beat. She hardly recognized him. Tall and straight. Hat pulled low. Pistol strapped around his waist. Saddle bags slung casually over his shoulder. Confident. Grown. He was the perfect picture of the man he so desperately wished to be. He stopped before her, removed his hat, and twisted the brim.

"Mother, I have to go now."

Six words. Six little words powerful enough to stop her heart. Anguish threatened to splinter her last shred of control. She reached out and pulled him close, clinging to him with unknown strength. Time stood still.

All too soon, they parted. She raised her face to meet his gaze and stared so intently into his bourbon colored eyes that she saw her reflection peering back at her. "You got everything? Shirts? Socks?"

"Yes, ma'am."

"Did you remember the wool blankets?"

"Yes, ma'am. I tied them on behind my saddle. But Mother you should keep yours. I only need one."

"Nonsense. Alice has more. You know how cold it gets at night. Oh! I almost forgot. Candles. I put a couple of candles and matches in your bag."

She watched a boyish grin spread across his face. "Mother, I seriously doubt I'll need candles."

"Trust me, Charlie. Sometimes a small bit of light

can make all the difference."

"Mother. I have to go."

Those words. A sad smile touched her lips. "No, Charlie, you don't. No one is forcing you. You want to go. You choose to go."

And I can't stop you.

She placed tender hands on either side of his face, tilted his head to her lips, and kissed his forehead, then each of his closed eyelids. "Charlie. Look at me."

His eyes came up to capture hers. Tears glistened at the corners.

"Listen to me. Never forget what I'm about to tell you. No matter where you go, no matter whom you become or what you'll have to do, remember this. I will always love you. Never doubt. Never forget."

He choked back a sob and swore. "I won't."

She felt him pull away, then watched him climb into his saddle.

With a nod toward her, Tom Carpenter and James Johnson eased their horses into line beside his. Alice walked to her side. Together they watched their first-born sons ride away from the safety of their arms. Long after the column of jingling boots and spurs disappeared, they stood in the dusty street. With false bravery they smiled weakly at one. Clara knew they would soon walk back into a life that was empty and without meaning.

Hidden in the shadows, Harvey Carpenter wiped at the single tear that inched down his grizzled face.

Heart as empty as his watch pocket, he stood.

Alone.

Old and alone.

Chapter 5

Jesse & Emmie

Jesse leaned his broad shoulders against the rough, wood wall and scowled. It was late, and Emmie was still in bed. She knew today was Sunday and how strict Ma was about church, yet she hadn't moved despite him yelling to get up, or else. The "else" being a switching from Ma. God, he hated Sundays. Hell and damnation day. The hooked-nosed Reverend Harris couldn't shout loud enough about the sins of man.

"Emmie! Get up! Don't make Ma come in here."

He was two steps away from dragging the covers off her when she struggled out from underneath them with turquoise flames shooting from her eyes.

"Don't! Don't take one more step! I'm up. Just 'cause you're nineteen, and you think you're the man of the house don't mean you can boss me."

Her pillow-veined face and mop of brownish-blonde ringlets that spilled down her back and flopped into her eyes made him laugh.

"Stop it! I'm not foolin'. I ain't in a good mood this morning."

"Noticed that." He couldn't resist the urge to tease. "Should I get the curry comb for your hair?"

"Jack ass!"

"What's got you so riled up this morning?"

"Well, for one thing, it's Sunday. That means church. I hate church. And that also means weasel-face Harris. I hate that ol' sin buster. Always yelling and hollering about our transgressions. He scares me. I'm only sixteen, how much sinning could I have done?"

"We ain't got time for wrongdoing. Now, get up. If Ma hears us talking about him, she'll skin us both."

"That's the other thing. I can't stand how she moons over him and hangs on every word he spouts about Old Scratch. She puts on this air, the perfect God-fearing woman, and he eats it up like a cat lapping up cream. I wonder what he'd think of her if he knew how two-faced she really is. How she beats—"

"Emmie, hush! If she hears ya, she'll take the belt to you for sure."

She rubbed the sleep from her eyes, and then mumbled. "Wouldn't be the first time."

He winced. That was true. Ma was heavy with the rod. Sometimes too heavy. His gaze fell on Emmie's right calf where the end of the strap had left its mark. That had been a night weeks ago, straight out of hell. He stepped in and tore the leather belt from Ma's hands before she beat Emmie to death. In horror he watched the blood run down Emmie's leg and spot the floor with crimson dots. How could Ma do such a thing? Emmie stood there with hurt and confusion welling in her eyes, but no tears. Not once did she cry or utter a sound. He'd gone to her room later that night, but she wasn't there. For a minute he feared she ran away but dismissed the thought. There was nowhere she could run. The hay loft was the only place she could go. The space over the stable had been his secret hiding place when he was younger, and in a moment of pity and brotherly love, he bequeathed it to her. He climbed the wood ladder leading to the fescue fortress and called out, "Emmie, you okay?"

"Go away!"

"No. I'm worried about ya. I won't come no closer, but I ain't leaving, even if I have to hang on this ol' ladder all night long."

"Oh, all right. Come on then. But don't talk to me."

He pushed a large bale to the side and stepped onto the landing. She sat huddled against a large block of yellowed hay, legs drawn up to her chest, arms folded around her knobby knees, rocking back and forth. She wouldn't look at him and shied from his touch.

"God, Emmie, I'm so sorry."

"Why? You didn't do nothing, except stop her. It ain't your fault she never hits you. It's me. I musta done something really bad for her to whoop me like that, but I can't figure out what it was."

"The only reason she never strapped me was because Pa was here then. She'd never lay a hand on you if he was here now. You didn't do nothing wrong."

When she turned her tear-stained face to his, he thought his heart would bust.

"Then why?"

Her simple question pierced his heart. Crossed-legged on the straw floor, he pulled a stem from a bale of hay. "I can't answer that. She swears she's sorry, and she'll never do it again."

"Do you believe her?"

"No."

"Me neither."

He chewed the stem, deep in thought. "Listen, Emmie. I don't know why she does it. But I do know it ain't your fault. You didn't do nothing wrong or bad. Maybe she's sick. She ain't acted right ever since Sammy was born. Maybe it has something to do with Pa leaving."

"She made him go. Why blame me? Jesse, I'm scared. What if she comes after me again and you ain't here to stop her?"

"Emmie, I'll always be here. I won't ever leave ya alone. Promise."

Ma hadn't touched her since then, but sometimes she got a crazed look in her eye. He wondered what would happen if he wasn't there, and like Emmie, the question, "why," still haunted him. It was hard to keep peace between them, and if Emmie didn't get up, he wasn't sure he could hold Ma off.

"Emmie, hurry!"

"Where's Ma?"

He glanced anxiously over his shoulder. "She's getting Sammy dressed. Why?"

She reached in under the bed and pulled out a small box.

"I don't want her to see this."

She took a tortoiseshell brush-and-comb set from the box and placed them on the bed. Her eyes, that just moments before had spit fire, now cooled and filled with emotion.

He smiled. "I wondered what you did with that."

"Don't be mad at me. I had to hide it. You know Ma would destroy it what with vanity being a sin and all. It's the best birthday present I ever got."

The urge to tell her the reason she felt that way burned on the tip of his tongue: it was the only birthday gift she had gotten. He'd worked hard for the money, chopping wood all winter long for the Widow Carlson, but it was worth it. He'd never forget the look of pure joy that crossed her face when he gave the set to her.

Ma worked her like a dog, but she hardly ever complained. Truth was, he felt sorry for her. His gaze traveled the room, and he sighed. A cot, threadbare blankets and thin pillow, a sad excuse for a bed. The floor was bare and cold and a blanket hung from the ceiling served as a bedroom door. She only had three dresses, and one was just to go to church in. Most of the time she went barefoot to save wear and tear on a pair of hand-me-down shoes. She deserved something nice.

"Aw, it ain't that much. Every girl should have something pretty especially on their sixteenth birthday. I see you looking at the other girls in church and the clothes they have."

"I ain't looking at their dresses. Most of them don't have much more than me."

"Then what are you looking at?"

"Their folks." She blushed. "They have mamas and daddies that love them. I know the Good Book says, 'Thou shalt not covet,' but I sure do wish Pa was still here and Ma…well," her voice wavered, "you know."

"Yeah, I know."

She brushed the curls from her face and grinned. Bright sparks of cobalt blue danced in her eyes, and her mood turned mischievous. "Good thing I got you to look after me then, ain't it? Besides, you don't have fine things, neither."

"That's different. A man don't need pretty things."

"A man?" She teased. "So, you *do* think you're the man of the house."

"That's right, and that man is telling you to hurry

up!"

He turned from her and smiled at the taunt she threw at his back.

"Yeah. Maybe. But you still ain't the boss of me."

Chapter 6

Jesse watched Emmie hanging back fussing with the ribbons that strained to corral her curly locks in their grasp. Why did girls take so long to get ready? "Come on, Emmie. We gotta hurry. If we're late for church, Ma will be madder than a foaming dog. You can fix your hair on the way, and watch out for the mud holes, it rained last night."

"Did she take Sammy?"

"Course not. We have to bring him. To save time, I'll carry him. Just hurry."

"If Pa had left at least one horse on the place, we wouldn't have to worry about being late. I get tired of walking everywhere."

Good point. Would be nice if there were a couple of horses in the barn, but Pa took all ten head when he rode out. He missed them. Missed Pa more.

A rabbit shot out of the tall grass and scampered across the muddy road in front of them. Sammy pointed a chubby finger at the cottontail and squealed.

Jesse laughed.

Emmie grunted.

Lord, she was touchy this morning. He side-stepped a mud puddle and shifted Sammy to his other arm. "Do you hate God?"

"What? Course not. I'm just mad at Him, that's all."

"Why?"

"He took Pa away."

That was the reason for her sour mood, she'd been thinking about Pa again. He'd been gone three years, but it seemed longer. Guilt pulled at him. He knew a lot more about the night Pa rode off than what he'd told her. Some things were better left unsaid. He figured it was for her own good. Maybe he should tell her. She was older now. He'd thought about it more than once, but it was hard to find the words, or the chance. Ma forbid them to even mention his name. The bitterness in her voice surprised him.

"You talk like he's dead. God didn't take him away. He left on his own."

"Why didn't God stop him? Why does He allow bad things to happen?"

Sammy squirmed in his arms and let out a fussy cry.

"You're holding him too tight. Give him to me. I'll carry him for a while."

He gladly handed Sammy to her and marveled at the way she tucked him in the crook of her arm and quieted him. She never failed to surprise him. One minute she could be a bobcat, spitting and hissing. The next, a gentle, loving young girl, shy as a fawn. She'd thought Pa hung the moon, and it broke her heart when he disappeared. She struggled to come to terms with it. Deep down his gut fluttered and he trembled. She wasn't the only one.

"Specks says God doesn't make bad things. He says it's in the Bible that God created everything, and it was good. He don't know bad 'cause He didn't make it."

"Who does Specks think made the bad things?"

"Us. We choose to do bad or good."

She cut him a quizzical look. "Specks said that? That's a good answer. Hard to believe Specks thought of it. He don't act like he's got sense to come in from the rain."

The hairs on the back of his neck bristled. Specks was his best friend, and he didn't like anyone talking bad about him. He'd excuse Emmie, however. She didn't have a close friend and didn't understand the bond of friendship.

"Oh, God. Jesse, look. We better hurry. Ma's waiting for us on the steps. She don't look none too happy, neither."

"She never does."

Jesse pulled at his too tight collar and took a quick look around to see if Specks was in church that morning. Becky Sue Thompson caught his gaze and gave him a syrupy smile. Heat crawled up the back of his neck. Becky was buck-teethed as a jack rabbit and just as homely, but her sister, Jenny was a real looker. Only problem was, she knew it. He doubted she even knew he was alive and had decided long before not to pursue her. Specks, on the other hand, worshipped the ground she walked on and was determined to win her hand someday.

The ferret-faced Reverend, Joel Harris, stepped to the pulpit, and the congregation hushed. Jesse searched the pews one last time for Specks. Where was he? He folded his hands in prayer and waited for the booming voice of the slicked-haired Reverend Harris to jolt the good folks of Calico Rock into confessing offenses they never even heard of. Most of them worked in the coal mines, and the only sin they were guilty of was wasting their lives away underground and underpaid. Very few had a pot-to-piss-in, but the yelling, screaming, Bible-punching Harris had a church with stained glass and a steeple tall enough to touch the floor of heaven. Was that heavenly righteousness?

Ma shot him a look so sour it would curdle milk, and his heart skipped. Had he said that out loud? He bowed his head and pretended to pray.

Ma was one of the church's most self-righteous patrons. How he hated her. It was because of her Pa had gone and left him to suffer the consequences. She blamed it on Pa's drinking, but he knew the real reason, and it had nothing to do with whiskey. The bitter taste of resentment stung the back of his tongue. He fought to choke the anger back into his gullet. Church was no place to harbor those kinds of feelings. Still, he felt powerless to stop them. Emmie wasn't the only one that thought Pa roped the moon. So had he. The truth about Pa's leaving seared him like a smoking brand, and he couldn't forget, no matter how hard he tried. He pushed the feeling deep into his soul, but emotions lurked in the darkness and waited. When he was silent like now, hatred raised its ugly head and bit. Ma was to blame for all their trouble. His stomach rolled and pitched as the memory came alive and swept him back into the turmoil of that night.

Thunder had rumbled across the sky and a jittery, eerie feeling hung heavy in the air. Sensing the uneasiness, the horses pawed the ground and milled in a circle. Storm clouds turned puke green and swirled around their cabin, what Pa called a twister sky. The approaching storm fed the tempest brewing between

Ma and Pa. He would never forget the hate in Ma's eyes or the words she spit in Pa's face.

"Don't come near me! Don't touch me ever again! Don't call me your pretty, Kentucky Filly either. That's all I am to you, ain't it? Just another one of your fancy brood mares. I never wanted children, and you knew it. I gave you a son, but I never asked for or wanted Emmie. I hate the sight of her, and I sure as hell don't want this one growing in my belly now."

The shock of those words squeezed his heart with a cold, hard fist. Without so much as a word, Pa turned and walked away. Nose pressed against his bedroom window, he'd watched in disbelief while Pa gathered the horses in the corral and saddled his. Panic raced up his spine. Pa couldn't be going. Not in the rain. Terrified, Jesse ran bare-foot into the damp and stood on shaky legs looking up at his icy stare. The wind whipped the trees and lightning ripped the sky. In the eerie light, Pa looked like the devil himself astride a pale horse.

"Pa?"

"Go back inside, son."

"Where ya going? You be coming back, won't ya? Take me with ya."

Hard lines softened but only for a moment, and Pa shook his head and gave a sad smile, but said nothing. The storm broke, and the downpour of rain soaked him. He scurried into the barn and watched Pa ride away into the wind and the dark. He'll be back. He's just going somewhere to sell the horses and simmer down. He won't leave us. He'll come home.

He never did.

Overnight Ma turned into a shrew of a woman.

Hatred and bitterness bleached the glow from her face, and dulled her silky hair to a tarnished shade of gold. She wore it captured into a severe knot at the back of her head, pulled so tight that it stretched her paper-thin skin across her bony cheekbones. She turned to religion for comfort, only to become a fanatic bending the Word of God to fit her purpose. Jesse couldn't stand what she'd become.

Ma was a hateful, nasty bitch.

Many times he thought about running away. He and Specks had gone so far as to make plans. Only one thing stopped him. A promise. He'd vowed to be there for Emmie. He couldn't leave her.

He never told Emmie about that night. Maybe the time had come for him to talk with her about what actually happened. An explanation would help her understand Ma's fits of rage. What words could he use to cushion the blow of Ma not wanting her? None came to mind.

His head jerked. Something was wrong. What was it? He breathed a sigh of relief. Was nothing. Church had ended, and the threats of fire and brimstone dissolved into the beams and rafters for another week. He looked around in a heavy-eyed daze. Ma wasn't there, but that wasn't a surprise. After the service she always cornered her beloved preacher-man to gush praises about his sermon. Emmie fussed with Sammy and glanced at the girls standing in back of the room.

When he saw them motion for her, he said, "You go on. I'll take Sammy off your hands for the afternoon. Hurry. They're waiting for you."

He didn't really want the job of watching Sammy, but the ghosts of that awful night had him caught in their grasp, and his heart went out to her. He lifted Sammy to his wide shoulders and ducked though the door. Sammy giggled with delight at the mock horse-back ride. Jesse blinked in the sunlight. Where was Specks? Loud laughter and heated words floated on the warm, high noon breeze, and he walked to the back of the church. Specks stood by the cemetery gate with clenched fists and blood in his eye.

Oh, lord, what had he walked into?

Chapter 7

"Whoa, Specks. What's wrong?"

"These yahoos called me a liar. I'm fixin' to clean their plows."

Specks' face was as red as his hair, and the freckles that dotted his forehead and cheeks jumped and danced in its fire. He looked like a puffed-up Rhode Island Red rooster, and if the situation hadn't been so tense, Jesse would've laughed. Jake Campbell *was* doubled over in a fit of laughter.

"Aw, come on, Jess," Jake said trying to catch his breath. "Specks claims he's gonna join the war. You should know better than all of us that he's blowing smoke. Remember the snipe hunt? He was so scared he just sat down in the middle of the woods and cried. If you hadn't gone in and pulled him out, he'd still be there clutching that gunny sack in his cold, gray hands. He ain't got enough guts to be a Johnny Reb."

Specks lunged and grabbed Jake by the shirt.

"You calling me a coward, too?"

Jake's cohorts closed like a pack of hungry wolves. Even though Specks towered over all of them, there was no way he could fight three on one.

Jesse swung Sammy from off his shoulders and sat him near the snake fence of the cemetery. He pushed his way into the circle and placed a ham hock of a hand on Jake's arm. Dark, hard eyes bore a hole in the bully's head.

"Naw. He ain't calling you nothing, Specks. Are ya, Jake?"

"Guess not." Jake lowered his gaze and fists. "I ain't got no quarrel with you, Jess. Come on, boys, let's go."

Jesse kept a wily eye on the three until they disappeared from sight. He hated the Jake Campbells of the world, smug bullies who picked on and poked fun at others to cover up their own short comings.

Specks turned and walked over to Sammy, then sank to the ground with a heavy sigh. "Jake's right. I am a yellow-belly. I thought I was going to die that night in the woods."

Jesse shook his head and sat cross-legged in the grass. The strong smell of honeysuckle drifted through the dogwood trees and tickled his nose.

"Being scared don't mean you're a coward. Besides, the way I remember it, the fog and frost moved in early that night. It's easy to get turned around in the mist and cold. You were only eight, and your ma had just died. Jake should've never played such a mean trick on you."

When Specks said nothing, Jesse knew something more than a childhood joke was bothering him. Whatever it was had to be serious. Specks was too happy-go-lucky and laid back to even think about hitting anyone.

"Specks, you okay?"

His friend grabbed a fistful of fallen pear blossoms and tossed them in the air. Sammy's eyes widened in delight as they fell like fragrant snowflakes around them. A slow, sheepish grin tugged at his lips.

"Should've known I couldn't fool you." His face clouded with uneasiness and his voice lowered.

"I ain't got nothing to live for. No purpose. I feel as lost as I was the night of the snipe hunt. Mama's been gone for ten years, and Pa's dead too, only he don't know it. He just wanders around from job to job, drinking his life away, living in the past. A man has to have a reason to get out of bed in the morning. I don't want to end up like Pa."

The sun played peek-a-boo with the clouds, but Jesse shivered in spite of its warmth. In a lot of ways his life mirrored Specks'. He lived day to day caught in the memory about how good it was when Pa was here and never dared to hope for anything better. He was stuck. That scared him. A sudden thought hit him.

"Is that why you're joining the war?"

"Yep. The South needs good soldiers, and I need to be needed. Seems like a perfect fit. Come with me, Jess."

What?

Was Specks loco? He couldn't leave, not with Emmie depending on him. Yet deep down, a longing pulled. Had to be more to life than a promise made in cold fear and heated turmoil.

The afternoon sun cast shadows on the ground of the tombstones, silent reminders of souls long departed. Branches on the pear trees that shaded their faces looked like hands folded in prayer. Cemeteries and markers were more for the living than the dead. The names chiseled in stone were constant reminders that loved ones did exist and their lives were important and meaningful. His lips hardened into a thin line. What would his headstone say?

Nothing. His life was blank.

Specks rose and kicked the ground in frustration. "I know by the look on your face what you're thinking. Hell's bells! Your ma ain't never goin' to change, and your pa won't be back. I dare you. Bury the past, right here and now. Come with me and make a new start."

"You know it ain't Ma. It's Emmie. I made a promise to her. I gave my word."

He watched disappointment darken Specks' face. Harsh reality was adventure's worst enemy.

The wind turned cool as the shank of the afternoon weakened the bite of the sun and shadows grew long and lanky. He should have been home hours ago.

"I gotta git. Ma will be wondering where I am. Listen. I ain't saying I won't go. It's just a big step to take. Have to smoke on it."

Specks' features brightened, and with renewed hope in his voice, he threw out a warning. "Don't take too long thinking about it. I'm leaving pretty quick."

Hours later, Jesse sat alone and wrestled with his conscience. With vacant eyes he watched the yellow glow of the lantern's light cast spider-veined shadows across the dirt floor of the rack-shambled barn. Should he go with Specks, or stay? What was the war about anyway? He didn't know. Kentucky couldn't make its mind up if it was north or south. So did a reason really matter?

Without conscience thought he reached into the feed can sitting beside him and tossed a fistful of corn to the banty rooster that was busy drilling the dirt with his sharp beak. Huh. He was that rooster. Day after mindless day, he scratched the earth only to end up with a handful of measly chicken feed. So wrapped in the memories of the way things used to be with Pa and the horses, he'd forgotten how to dream. All he wanted from the time he could say the word horse, was a ranch of his own. Trapped in the tedious routine of what his life had become, bitterness festered in his gut, bubbled and churned. The war was an opportunity. A way out. Freedom.

But at what price?

Sammy was too young, wouldn't even know or care that he was gone.

Ma? Lord, how he struggled with his feelings about her. A son should honor and love his mother. It was a sin not to, wasn't it? He had—once. But no longer.

Emmie would suffer the most. He loved Emmie. She could be stubborn as a mule when she knew she was right or had her mind made up, but she was as loyal as a hound dog, and her innocence softened her rough edges. In her eyes, he could do no wrong. She knew him better than he knew himself and loved him for who he was. How could he live with himself knowing he placed her in harm's way?

His boot slammed into the side of the feed bin. He shouldn't have to choose. Anger clawed him with scarlet talons, and he grabbed the pitchfork and jabbed the forks into the hay.

Damn it. This shouldn't be his problem. Why did the innocent always suffer the sins of the guilty?

He carried the wounded lump of hay to Bessie's stall, tossed it into the manager with a careless flip. Most of the straw dropped rudely at the feet of the one-horned milk cow who snorted a hot breath of displeasure. He ignored her, returned to the feed box, and fumbled in his pocket for his tobacco. With deliberate care he tapped the tangy leaves between the folded paper then ran his tongue down the edges to seal the smoke closed. He struck a match and blew out the flame, drew a deep breath and held it in his lungs until the taste weakened.

The cigarette's smoky signature scribbled aimlessly through the air. His head cleared. Wasn't right to put his life on hold for a promise made in the heat of the moment? Wasn't reasonable to believe he could always shield Emmie from hurt. Sooner or later she would have to learn to stand on her own. Depending on him only made life that much harder. If he didn't get out of here, he would rot. In order to save himself he would have to go.

Emmie burst through the door with steel darts shooting from her eyes, and his resolve buckled.

Nothing could make telling her he was leaving an easy job.

Chapter 8

"Where the Sam Hill have you been? I had to do your chores 'cause you were nowhere to be found. What's the matter with you?"

"Don't bow-up at me, little Miss Priss. Nothing's wrong. Can't a man have a smoke and some quiet time to himself?"

"Don't try and hornswoggle me. Smoking in the barn is the biggest sin since Eve gave the apple to Adam. If Pa was here, he'd bust you a good one."

He threw the smoldering butt to the dirt and ground the end under his boot heel. A deep frown wrinkled his forehead and a low growl escaped him, then he spoke. "Well, he ain't here, is he?"

In defiance he pulled the makings from his pocket and rolled another cigarette. "And I'll smoke anywhere I damn well please."

"Who put the burr under your saddle? Specks?"

He whirled on her. "Specks don't have nothin' to do with this. I'm just sick and tired of this place, Ma, and everything."

"Me too?"

Her injured look cooled the heat of his anger, and he grimaced. "No, course not. Sorry. I just miss Pa and how it used to be. Nothing will ever be the same."

His head throbbed, and he closed his eyes to shut out the glare of harsh reality. In that brief reprieve, he stood as a young boy again, and the smell of leather and hay, saddle soap and liniment surrounded him. He became lost in the memory.

"Remember what it was like before Pa left? We laughed all the time. Couldn't wait for mornings to come so I could help him with the horses. This barn was full of the finest horseflesh in Kentucky. People bragged that he was the best trainer in the state. Remember?"

Bessie stomped the dirt and snorted for attention. Emmie reached over the cracked stall gate and rubbed the cow's wet nose.

"I...I remember that bay mare and her baby."

"I remember her!" Jesse slapped his leg. "Pa called her Belle and her colt, Tag because he was always tagging along after his mama." He paused and took a long drag from his cigarette. His gaze fell on the broken stalls. What a shame. The farm was dying a slow death, and like black-winged buzzards, the rancid odor of despair and surrender circled the decaying wood and waited for the rattle of its last breath.

"Emmie, this place is as empty as I feel. I hate it here."

"You're not alone, I do too. But it was Pa's drinking that caused it. Ma would've never made him go if he had stopped."

The cigarette dangled from his lip and almost fell to the ground.

"Is that what she told you? Do you really believe that?"

"Well, what did happen? If it weren't his drinking that changed everything, what did?"

The moment of truth was here. Now was the time

to tell her the real reason behind Pa's leaving, but he wasn't sure of what to say. He paced the row of stalls and glanced up at the barn's slumping shoulders. A startled swallow swooped from the rafters, and he ducked as it flew past his head and out the door.

"Sammy happened, that's what."

She scoffed. "Sammy? He's just a baby."

"That's the problem. Ma didn't want more young'uns."

"What the hell are you talking about?"

"I heard her tell Pa the night he rode out."

"Tell me."

"It don't matter. Just take my word for it and know it had nothing to do with liquor."

"Tell me!"

Damn! Hard-headed as a mule.

"You're stubborn as an ol' Billy Goat, you know that?"

Her eyes locked him in a deep, dark stare and he sighed. "Ma told him she didn't marry him just to be his brood mare."

"What's that mean?"

"It means just for having babies. Understand?"

"Like Belle?"

"Yeah. Like that."

He watched her slump to the ground and lean her boney back against Bessie's stall gate. Her face squirmed, and his breath caught waiting for the next question.

"Was she…was she talking just about Sammy?"

"No. I'm sorry, Emmie. I know it ain't an easy thing to hear. It ain't an easy thing to say, neither."

"Explains a lot, though."

Her head dipped and long eyelashes slipped over her lids.

Moths gathered around the lantern's flickering flame and cast bat-sized shadows against the weathered wood of the barn. He watched as she marked patterns in the dust with her bare toes and his heart wrenched. The broken stalls, empty corrals, and hollow barn were mirror imagines of his dented soul. He had no hope, and without purpose, life wasn't worth living. He'd made up his mind, he was going with Specks. But he'd rather face a nest of rattlers then tell her. His back stiffened and he opened his mouth, but the words stuck in his windpipe. He cleared his throat, and his voice grated his gullet like sandpaper against rough wood.

"Emmie. I'm leaving."

At first he thought she hadn't heard. Then he saw her chest rise as she took-in a quick breath.

"Leaving? What are ya talking about?"

"The war." He struggled to keep his voice calm but it wavered just the same. "Specks and me are leaving to join the war."

"Specks!"

She leaped from the floor and stood belligerently in front of him.

"That red-headed string bean?" Sarcasm dripped from her tongue like snake venom.

"That figures. He can't put his shirt on without you there to button him up. And you…you let him lead you around like you got a ring in your nose."

God. She could piss him off quicker than anyone he knew, even Ma. Anger burned up his spine, and he turned from her.

"Ma won't let ya!" She yelled at his back.

He wheeled back and laughed in her face.

"I ain't telling her. One day I'll be here, the next I won't."

"Just like Pa."

Her accusation hit like a hammer, and his temper flared. He shoved her backward.

"Damn it! It ain't like Pa at all."

Her fists clenched.

" 'Tis too, and you know it. He took the easy way out and ran like a scalded dog. And you are too."

Her words stopped him cold.

"What's that supposed to mean? Emmie, do you hate Pa for leaving?"

"Maybe." Her chin lifted, and she met his gaze straight on. "I mean...I don't hate him. But he slipped off in the night without telling me good-bye or that he was sorry. He could've stayed and at least tried to fix things with Ma instead of sneaking off in the dark like a thieving coward."

"He did try, Emmie."

"How? With whiskey? Drinking don't fix nothin'."

"Guess he was tired."

"Well, maybe Ma was too. Did he ever think of that? Could be that's what she was talking about when she said she didn't want more babies."

His voice hardened. "You taking her side now?"

"Jack ass. I ain't takin' no one's side. All I know is that the men of this house ain't actin' like men. All of ya are running away from your problems and leaving me to clean up the mess. It ain't my job. Besides, I'm only sixteen. I don't know how."

She stood breathless before him. Tears welled in her eyes and sparked the ones in his. Deep down she was just a scared girl, how could he be angry with her? He sighed and reached for her fists. His voice lost its steely edge.

"Emmie, I remind her of Pa. If I'm not here, things will be better. You'll see."

"Take me with ya."

Her quick change in mood surprised him and her enthusiasm made him laugh.

"Take you? Oh Emmie, that's funny."

Immediately she challenged him. "What's so funny about it?"

"You're a girl."

"So? I can outride most men, and I'm tough. I'm tall and skinny, and if I cut my hair I'll look like a boy. We can tell everyone that I'm your kid brother."

Good God. He couldn't believe what she was saying. Exasperated he shook his head. He hadn't bargained on this. She was stubborn enough to follow him, and he had to nip this idea of hers in the bud.

"Emmie, you ain't going, and that's final. If you follow me, I'll hate you the rest of your life. War is no place for a girl, and I'm ordering you to stay home."

Her silence was deafening. Damn. Should've never said such cruel words, but what if she got killed looking for him. He'd never forgive himself. He flicked his cigarette to the ground and stomped off toward the house.

Emmie stood in the darkness alone and heartbroken. Crushed by his harsh words, she dropped to the ground and buried her head in her arms. The stars witnessed her tears and the half-moon wrapped around her shoulders, giving neither warmth nor sympathy. In the distance an owl asked the question, "Hooo?"

She picked up his discarded cigarette, took a deep pull from it, and mocked the wise bird. "That jack ass brother of mine, that's who."

How could he leave her? Silent tears slid down her cheeks and hit the ground splashing her bare feet like dirt-covered raindrops. He'd made fun of her for being a girl, like being female was a weakness or a sin. It hurt to know that he thought of her that way.

Damn him. No matter what he'd said she sure wasn't gonna stay here without him.

With a vengeance she jabbed the smoldering paper into the ground and took the Lord's name in vain.

"God Dammit! I hate this place!"

Chapter 9

Emmie raced downhill to the creek. Ma's ranting and raving chased after her, and she urged her legs to pump faster. The water bucket clutched in her hand banged against her knee, and she crashed to the ground with a loud thud. The bucket flew from her hands and smacked the side of a Sycamore tree. The crisp sound of splintering wood echoed through the air. For a heartbeat, both she and the pail lay broken and still. Deep sobs finally broke the eerie silence and shook her frame like a scrawny ragdoll.

Jesse had been gone for a week, and Ma was punishing her for his disappearance. From sunrise to sunset she worked. Chopping wood. Hauling water. Milking. Cooking. Cleaning. Mothering Sammy.

Ma just sat and read the Bible.

She struggled to her feet and limped over to the water bucket, a heap of twisted metal bands and dislocated wood. Damn. She would have to climb the hill and find another pail. Stiff and sore, she trudged up the path to the cabin. Her skinned knees burned, and her cotton dress hung like a death shroud on her thin shoulders. It was only fitting. She was dead inside.

"Emmie? You fetch that water yet? Where have you been? Land sakes! You're as worthless as that no-good brother of yours."

Anger stung her tongue. Ma was in a bad humor

and mouthing off wouldn't help anything.

"I had to come back for another bucket. The old one broke."

"Go then. Be quick about it! Take Sammy with ya, I'm tired of hearing him cry."

"Aw, Ma, can't he stay here? It's too hard to haul water and carry him at the same time. Besides, he has a fever and ain't feeling good."

"Ain't nothing wrong with him. Just puny. Give him a wet rag to chew on. Quit standing there. Get the water."

Might as well have said, "Throw the dog a bone," for all the love and concern in her voice.

Bone-weary, Emmie leaned over to lift Sammy from the floor. A sharp pain jabbed her back and burned up her spine. She fought against the tears that pushed against her eyelids. Ma sure as hell wouldn't see her cry.

"Emmie! Now!"

Something inside snapped.

"What ya want first, Ma? Which one? Tell me. The water? The wood? The milk? The cookin'? The cleanin'? But don't you fret none, I'll get it done. You just sit there and read the Good Book. Maybe it'll tell ya how to get these chores done. Your precious Reverend Harris and his church is all that matters to you, ain't it? Well, all your Bible readin' and holier-than-thou ways won't get this work done. It won't bring your men back to ya neither."

The slap came so quick and hard she didn't have time to block it. The bitter taste of blood flavored her lips.

"You hush, little girl." Esther hissed like a

cornered possum. "You ain't got your big brother to step between us now. You've sassed me for the last time. I'm gonna wear you raw."

Emmie's blood chilled. Ma trapped her between the kitchen wall and table. With cat-like speed she lunged at Emmie.

The table overturned.

Tin cups and plates clattered to the floor.

Sammy screamed.

Emmie threw her hands in front of her face to ward off another blow.

Unable to strike skin, Esther grabbed Emmie's long hair and twisted. She dragged Emmie kicking and yelling across the kitchen floor to the door.

"Ma! Don't! I'm sorry!"

Esther kicked the door open with one foot and flung her to the ground like a pan of dirty dishwater.

"Get out! Get out of my sight! Don't come sneakin' back, neither!"

Emmie feared for her life.

Half crawling, half standing, she regained her feet and ran to the only safe haven she knew, the hay loft.

Her legs shook so bad they didn't want to work.

She slipped on the ladder's rungs and banged her skinned knees against its hard wood.

Dammit!

Pain shot through her like a red-hot poker, and she clung to the steps in stunned limbo. With sheer will she struggled to the top of the landing. Ma never stepped foot in the barn, but now wasn't the time to take chances. The straw bales were heavy boulders, and her neck and shoulders tingled with pain when she pulled and stacked them into a fort of bluegrass and fescue.

Drenched with sweat, she slumped against her straw fortress. Her heart pounded. The imprint of Ma's hand burned like a brand on the side of her face.

Never had she seen Ma so angry. Her red-rimmed eyes bore the look of a rabid animal.

Ma was plumb loco.

What was she going to do? There was no one to turn to for help. The only one that cared was Jesse, and he abandoned her.

Damn him.

When Pa rode away, she vowed never to love anyone that much again. But Jesse was different, and she needed someone to care, so she reached out to him. Look where that got her. Never again. Never would she trust anyone, ever again. She didn't need them anyway.

Tears called her a liar.

Chapter 10

The full moon hung high in the night sky. Long beams leaked through the slats in the barn's weary walls and offered just enough light to keep Emmie from sitting in total darkness. Familiar night sounds bounced off the empty stalls and landed beside her. Beneath her, Bessie chewed her cud, and chickens clucked themselves to sleep in nests of dimpled straw. A coyote yipped in the distance.

She couldn't hide forever.

Do something.

Move.

On wobbly legs she climbed down from the loft, headed for the door, and peeked around its side. There was no light from the cabin. Good. Ma and Sammy must be asleep. On feet silent as cat paws, she crossed the yard and opened the cabin's door. The creak of rusty hinges made her heart jump. She spit on them to quiet their protest.

Her heart beat fast. Breath came in short, rapid gasps.

Quiet. Must be silent.

She willed her breath to calm and waited for her eyes to adjust to the darkness of the cabin's insides. Thank God for the full moon's light.

Softer than a sigh, she bypassed her room and went directly to Jesse's. With shaking hands she unbuttoned the thin dress and let it slide to the floor. She grabbed a shirt and a pair of trousers from the wardrobe and pulled them on. They would do.

Grab one more pair for good measure, his old felt hat, and ragged boots. Take a blanket from the bed. The nights are cool.

On tiptoes she crossed to her room. The only thing she wanted was the brush and comb set that Jesse gave her. Even though, at that moment, she was furious with him, she knew deep down that the feeling would pass. She wasn't about to leave his special gift behind for Ma to smash to bits.

In the kitchen she pulled a flour sack from behind the stove and stuffed her belongings into it. A fresh loaf of bread sat on the counter. She tore a piece from it and crammed it in her mouth. She wrapped the loaf in another flour sack and put it in her poke. Water was easy to find, but food was a different matter. Have to think smart.

There was only one thing left to do. With her sack slung over her shoulders, she quietly left the house and headed back to the barn.

With trembling hands she lit the lantern in the stable and stood in its dim glow. In all of her sixteen years, she'd never cut her hair, and it streamed down her back like a waterfall of honey and gold. Her curly mane was the only pretty thing about her, and she eyed the shears like they were tools of the devil. Her hand shook when she picked them up and pulled her hair forward to meet the blades.

No.

Eyes squeezed shut, she argued with herself.

Just cut it. You have to. You gotta look like a boy.

No. It's too pretty.

It's just hair. It'll grow back.

No. I can't. Besides, it's a sin for a woman to cut her hair.

Oh, who am I foolin'? So far I've coveted my neighbor's families, taken the Lord God's name in vain, and dishonored my mother. The fires of hell don't burn any less hot for one sin or twenty. Cut it.

Dishonored my mother? What happened to the commandment that says, "Honor thy sons and thy daughters?"

That's a good question. Bet ol' hook nose can't answer that one. Quit stallin'. Cut it.

Dammit.

She grabbed the long locks and hacked at them.

Fast.

Furious.

Frantic.

Tears glistened on her cheeks.

Don't think.

Hair swirled in the air like dandelion wisps and floated to her feet.

Keep cutting.

Sobs tore at her throat.

Don't stop.

Oh, God.

She flung the shears to the ground.

There.

It was done.

Trembling fingers inched up her neck to her ears and pulled at the short, choppy strands. With numb disbelief she crumbled to the dirt and ran her hands through the severed curls that lay stagnant and dull in the barnyard filth.

Sweet Jesus. What had she done? Ma would beat her to death.

Ma.

Her lips straightened into a thin, hard line, and she gained her feet. The heel of her boot came down hard. She stomped the locks deep into the earth, burying them and her past forever.

Ma would never hurt her again.

No longer would she allow others to rule her life. From now on she answered only to herself. God pity anyone that got in her way. Wherever Jesse was, she would find him and fight beside him.

She began to run.

You're runnin', just like Pa.

No, I ain't. Pa ran away. I'm running toward.

The moonlight was her guide. Determination was her courage.

Whisperings

"Shut up! Shut up! Shut up!"

The voices in my head are driving me nuts. I scream at Charlie and Jesse who bombard me with images, thoughts, and feelings, 24-7. Time has no meaning to ghosts, but I'm not a spirit. I work for a living. It's exhausting to type until 2:00 in the morning, then get up at 6:00, go to work and be coherent.

I can't take a shower without them popping in with their thoughts. One night I got in and out of the bath three times to write down the brilliant sentences and dialogue they speak. I waddle down the hall like a terry-clothed duck to get to my computer. Finally, I get smart and put a writing tablet and pencil by the tub.

I'm a menace behind the wheel. On auto-pilot from home to work, I weave in and out of traffic while fighting the Civil War in my head.

On the job, half of my brain inputs important data while the other half thinks about format and story plot. Ironically, I make fewer mistakes this way than when I'm fully present and focused on the paperwork. Thank God. Even so, this can't continue. I'm pooped.

Can you give ghosts an ultimatum? I was about to find out.

"Okay, boys, I realize you have a lot to say and now that you have a captive audience, the floodgates are open. But I'm only human and rules need to be established. So, here's what's going to happen: Come to me only when I say it's time or I can't continue."

They grudgingly comply, but "temper tantrum" flashes in my mind's eye.

News Bulletin: Ghosts have a sense of humor.

~R. H. Burkett

Chapter 11

The Lieutenant

Peter James Montgomery slowed his big dun gelding to a smooth jog-trot and took in a deep breath of the clean, sharp smell of pine. The warmth of the Georgia sun thawed four years of New York's harsh winds and icy winters to a dull memory.

The sound of baying hounds reached his ears and announced his arrival. Anxiety shot though him. The thought of seeing Father again caused unresolved anger to churn in his stomach. Father had sent him to West Point to get rid of him.

The first year at the Academy was unbearable, the first time he'd ever been away from home. Homesick, he'd struggled to fit in with the fast pace of the East, unfamiliar accents, and pre-conceived notions that all Southern people were ignorant and ill-bred. Resentment toward Father festered, and by the time he graduated, the bitterness had turned into full-blown hatred. For Mother's sake he would keep a tight rein on his anger, but the thought of facing Father infuriated him.

"Peter?"

His heart quickened, and he pulled the dun to a quick halt.

Mother.

She glided across the manicured lawn in a gentle

swoosh of turquoise skirts and cream-colored petticoats. Stepping down from the saddle, he ran to meet her and gathered her in his embrace. Then leaning back, his eyes misted at the sight of her while she smothered him with joyful tears and kisses.

"Oh, Peter. You're home at last. I've missed you more than you will ever know."

She backed away and studied him with sapphire eyes and sweeping lashes.

"I declare, is that stubble I see on your cheeks? And I know you've grown a foot taller."

She shook her head in wonder. "You left my side a young boy of eighteen, and today you return a man. Everyone is so excited about your homecoming. Sarah is beside herself. It's all she's been talking about for weeks. Ruby made her a new dress in honor of your arrival. Be sure to mention how pretty she looks."

He smiled. Virginia Rutherford Montgomery was a rose among thorns. Tall and graceful, polite and genteel, her heart beat with compassion and selfless giving. Always the lady, she was the perfect Southern Belle. But he wondered if she was living a lie. He suspected she detested Father as much as he did.

"Sarah was only six when I left. I'm surprised she remembers me."

"How could she forget her big brother? You were the only one that took her riding." A hint of sarcasm edged her words. "God knows her father wouldn't dream of taking time out of his day for her."

"Virginia. Get out of the way. Quit babying the boy."

Peter tensed at the sound of Father's booming voice. With wily eyes he watched the big man stride toward him and gritted his teeth.

"Father, it's good to be home."

"Union Blue? I'll not have it."

Inside Peter bristled, but on the outside he smiled and answered with a level voice. "Father, I've just graduated from West Point, which, if I remember correctly, was your desire. I'm a proud officer of the United States of America. What other uniform should I be wearing?"

The remark would irk Father, and he suppressed a smug look of satisfaction when anger spread across his face.

"Don't play me for a fool. You know damn well the United States has turned its back on the South. No respecting Southern family would be caught dead wearing heathen blue, and I command you to take it off."

Peter stiffened. Time hadn't changed Father. Why had he thought it would? The bullying, pompous son-of-a-bitch.

"Father, the South hasn't seceded as yet and until it does, if ever, I see no reason to remove this uniform."

"Peter! Peter!"

He glanced up at the cry and smiled while Sarah flew across the yard with strawberry curls that bounced with every step. Laughter tagged after her like a faithful pup. She threw herself in his arms.

Words poured from her mouth and in one long breath she exclaimed, "Peter, I'm so glad you're home. I've waited a long time and have so much to show you. Dixie has four kittens, and Mother says I can keep them all. Will you take me riding? I'm learning to play the piano. Want to hear?"

He hugged her close and kissed the top of her head. Love and gratitude overwhelmed him. Her arrival diffused a volatile situation, and he sighed in relief when Father turned from him and grunted.

"Virginia, I've important business in town. I expect supper when I return."

He turned back and glared.

Peter met his fierce look with causal indifference.

"Don't be wearing that uniform when I return. I won't have my son stinkin' of Yankee blue."

Peter sat Sarah on the ground and watched his father stride toward the stables. Sarah grabbed his hand and led him toward the house, talking non-stop. He laughed but kept one eye trained on Father's retreating figure. West Point stressed the importance of keeping your friends close, but your enemies even closer. Mother was correct, he wasn't a boy anymore.

Father needed to tread with care.

Chapter 12

"Master Peter, it's good to have you home."

Peter broke into a wide smile and pulled the gray-haired butler to his chest.

"Toby. It's wonderful to see you." He hugged the man with affection. "How many times have I told you not to call me Master?"

Toby backed away and a possum-grin spread from ear to ear.

"I reckon' about every time I calls you that, suh." He shook his wooly head. "Hmm, hmm. Just looks at you. You've spouted up into quite a man."

"You ol' fool." The voice came from upstairs. "You don't know what you're talkin' about. He's skinnier than a split-rail fence."

Peter laughed and took two steps toward her as Ruby hurried down the stairway and threw her meaty arms around his neck.

"Ruby, you're a sight for sore eyes. It's good to see you. Please tell me you're still doing the cooking around here. I've been dreaming of your chicken and dumplings ever since I left New York."

Her bear paw of a hand smoothed his coat, and she fussed over him like a mother hen. "I sures do, and in honor of your homecoming we'll have them dumplings tonight for supper."

"My mouth's watering as we speak. How's

Amos?"

Toby beamed with pride at the sound of his son's name. "He's fourteen now and growin' like a weed. Spends mosts of his time down at the stables. I'll have him fetch your horse."

"Thanks, Toby. Tell him to take extra care of Major. He's carried me a long way."

Ruby patted him on the shoulder. "I best be gettin' into the kitchen and seein' to that chicken." She paused and threw him a wink. "It's good to have ya home."

Peter climbed the staircase to his room and trailed his fingertips across the smooth mahogany wood of the banister. Yes, it *was* good to be back. He'd missed Mother's gentleness, Sarah's youthful enthusiasm, and the friendship of Toby and Ruby.

At the top of the landing he peered at the rooms below. Big and pretentious. Like Father. His jaw clenched. Father. Why did Mother marry him? He had his suspicions. Maybe it was time to voice them.

He unbuttoned his coat and hung it with care in his closet. Long fingers smoothed the shiny buttons and lieutenant's bars on the collar. The insignia represented four long years of hard work and dedication. Pride made his chest swell.

Father could go to hell.

A slight smile crossed his chiseled face, and he walked downstairs to the back porch.

The strong smell of honeysuckle greeted him when he opened the door to the verandah. Mother sat fanning herself even though it was early spring and not yet hot. A pitcher of lemonade and a decanter of bourbon sat on the wicker table beside her. He poured a glass of lemonade and chuckled.

"I see Ruby still insists on mixing oranges in with the lemons."

"It's her secret ingredient. She claims that even though the two are different, they're still fruit and can work together to produce a better, sweeter taste."

"Ruby is a wise woman." He smacked his lips and grinned.

Crossing over to the porch steps he sat down, leaned his back against the railing, and pulled his pipe from his vest pocket.

"Peter? I didn't know you smoked."

"Picked the habit up at school, I'm afraid. It helped pass the time. If it offends you, I'll put it out."

"No. It doesn't upset me. I'm just surprised, that's all. Truth be known, I rather fancy the smell of good pipe tobacco. Your grandfather smokes a pipe, and it brings back fond memories of my childhood at Ravenswood."

"How is Grandfather?" He lit the pipe and watched her face sadden through the smoke.

"He's doing well. I haven't seen him in quite some time. I imagine he's lonely all by himself in that big house of his. I see him in your eyes. You have his temperament and style."

"Pity I don't have his name as well."

"Peter."

He changed the subject. "What's this important business Father has in town?"

"Oh, I'm sure it's about the war." The charm of her soft, southern drawl did little to hide her irritation. "That's all he talks about now days. It's all anyone talks about, for that matter. I grow so weary of it."

He looked hard at her. Even in sorrow and worry

she was beautiful. No wonder Father claimed her as his young bride. However, Grandfather's money hadn't hurt. Her beauty was only icing on the cake.

"Peter, why do you frown so? You're much too young to be so serious."

"It's this suggestion of war, Mother. I pray it's only talk and nothing more. I studied battle at the Academy, and I don't want any part of it."

"Ah, yes, the Academy." A faint smile softened her face. "Your father claimed West Point would make a man out of you, but I knew he only wanted to separate you from my overprotective arms. I will never forgive him for sending you away."

Her confession caught him off guard. "I was lonely, at first. But I adjusted and made strong friendships." He sighed. "War will make enemies out of the very men I called friends. I love this country and don't want it torn apart over a way of life that is past its prime."

She folded the fan in her lap and circled the lip of the crystal water glass with long, nervous fingers. "Peter, I'm afraid that your father will never agree with you."

"That's what I'm talking about, Mother. This war will pit father against son, brother against brother. No one will win."

"Calm yourself, son. You don't have to convince me. I understand."

He drew in a long breath and waited for the soothing vanilla tobacco to ease the turmoil rumbling in his chest. "Do you, Mother? I think not. No one knows the horror of battle until it's too late."

"Do you know just how destructive man can be?

76

From the beginning of time, since Cain and Abel, man kills. Man destroys. The excuses are many but can be boiled down to only four. Hate. Fear. Jealously. Greed."

"The Crusades killed in God's name." Pipe smoke circled the porch like a thin spiced ribbon, and his voice grew thick. "Christians, whose main doctrine is peace and love, whose own commandments condemn killing as a sin, invaded a country and slaughtered its people. Why? Fear. Those *heathens* dared to worship a God that just might be more powerful than ours, so we destroyed them. How ironic that our forefathers fought for freedom of religion, yet we persecute others because they choose to call the Lord by a different name. As if that matters. God is God, no matter the name."

He lifted his gaze to the sky. "Sometimes I wonder what He thinks of that."

"Peter, again you've surprised me. I had no idea you were so philosophical."

A sad smile touched his lips. "The Romans weren't any better. They enslaved their captives and made them fight, not only themselves, but wild animals as well. Lions. Tigers. In large arenas while they watched. For entertainment. What madness is that?"

He searched her face for an answer, but found none.

"Mother, I don't want war. The South won't win. Not because the North has better generals or armies. Which it does. And not because it has more money or men. Which it does. But because the South fights for the wrong reasons. Slavery. Immorality. Arrogance and greed. Those motives didn't work for the Crusades or the Romans, and won't work for the South. And it shouldn't. For it is wrong."

"Careful, son." Her warning came as a whisper and sent chills up his spine. "There are many that would say you speak treason. Your father being one."

He laughed. "You didn't raise a fool, Mother. I speak these words only to you. I'm very much aware that some men would think them weak, cowardly. This is only a conversation between a mother and her son on a spring day in late afternoon."

His smile turned mischievous. "Sometimes I think the world would be a better place if ruled by mothers."

"Oh, Peter, now you speak blasphemy. What a silly notion."

Her ridicule ruined his playfulness, and he lost himself in melancholy. "And if by some cruel twist of fate, the South prevailed, what grand prize would we win? A nation, bruised, battered, bleeding, and coming apart at the seams. Scarred forever." He turned to her.

"Do you honestly believe that men such as Father, who has no comprehension of the word compassion, would be able to heal those scars and mend the people? *That* is blasphemy, Mother."

Behind him the melodious tones of Beethoven drifted from the parlor's window and added ironic harmony to the battle raging in his soul. "My, lord. Is that Sarah at the piano? She plays with such passion."

Virginia smiled. "Yes, your father insists she behave like a lady at all times. I think she channels her aggressions into her music."

Peter gazed into the garden that surrounded the verandah. Sadness edged his words. "War will end the music. It's coming. I smell it in the air as thick as the honeysuckle and magnolia that drapes this porch on sultry, summer nights. Only, not a sweet smell, but the stink of decay, deception, and death."

His eyes closed and his fists clenched.

"I'm a son of the South, and she is a demanding mother. Even though sympathetic to the North, Mama Dixie will insist on my allegiance. I'm an officer and will be called to command. Mostly boys, I fear. War always takes the young first. I'll be responsible for their very lives." His shoulders slumped.

"I fear the task is too great. How can I save them, Mother? It frightens me to my very core."

"Son." Her voice came soft. "If war happens, you'll not be responsible for it or over who lives or dies. That is God's decision. But today there is no war. Why worry over something that may never occur and that you have no control over if it does? Your compassion for your fellow man swells my heart with pride."

He whirled.

"Compassionate? Do not think me so. Like it or not, Father's cold blood runs in my veins. If threatened. If pushed. I'm more than capable of violence. Hard and premeditated, if need be."

Thunder rumbled in the distance. A storm brewed and rain clouds ushered in not only a change in the weather, but in his attitude as well. The air crackled with tension and a dark, uneasiness swirled with the wind. Lightning flashed and so did his eyes.

"Does Father still beat you?"

Chapter 13

Virginia's glass hit the wood floor and shattered. The fan fell and landed in the pool of lemonade. Water soaked through the paper, and tiny rainbows of paint ran off and trailed across the porch. All color drained from her expression as well.

"How do you know that?"

Peter bit his lip and swiped at the tears that gathered in the corners of his eyes. He'd made a guess. One he wished had been wrong. "I didn't for sure. You just confirmed it."

Sarcasm laced her words. "Well played, my young Lieutenant. Little wonder you excelled in tactics at West Point. Of course it helped that you caught me unaware, but I never thought my own son would wish to trick me so."

"Would you have told me any other way?"

"I suppose not."

"You didn't answer the question. Does he still hit you?"

"Not for a long time, now."

Peter drew a deep breath. "How long? Four years?"

"About that…." She gasped. "Oh, God. Peter, it has nothing to do with you."

"Why did you marry him?"

He watched ribbons of scarlet creep up her neck and wash over her face. She reached for the bourbon on the whicker table and refused to meet his glare. "My relationship with your father is none of your business." She poured the whiskey into a glass.

"You had no choice, did you? You were with child. It's my fault..."

"Peter. Stop. Listen to me. You are not to blame. How could you think such a thing? I love you and Sarah more than anything in this world. I'd marry the devil himself for you and her. I beg you. Quit this interrogation. My life is my choice, and I have no regrets."

He watched her drain the shot of bourbon in one gulp. She lied. To protect him, she lied. And he never loved her more.

"Son, you don't understand your father. He isn't a bad man. He did the honorable thing by marrying me. He saved my family from shame. I owe him that."

Thunder roared, split the sky, and matched Peter's fury.

"God damn it! Mother! Stop! Why do you defend him so? Your dowry made him a rich man. Rutherford money secured his position in southern society. It bought this plantation and stables of horses. Honorable? It wouldn't surprise me to learn that he tricked you into his bed."

His eyebrows arched at the ease with which she swallowed another glass of whiskey. She said nothing. Didn't have to. Her actions confirmed his suspicions.

"You owe him nothing. I hate him. Everything about him makes me sick. His face. Voice. The way he pushes you aside like you're invisible. I'm ashamed to be his son, to carry his name."

She wheeled and threw the glass at his feet.

"Peter. Enough! He is still your father, and I will not tolerate this kind of talk. Do you understand me?"

The shock of her scolding cooled his anger. His back straightened.

"I hear you. But know this. You and Sarah are the most important people in my life, and *I* will not *tolerate* any of his threats aimed at you or her. I vow, as God is my witness, if he ever strikes you again, I'll kill him. Do *you* understand *me*?"

Time stretched for an eternity between them.

The sound of barking dogs came from the front of the house and broke the silence. He watched her chin lift and the mask of compliance fall into place.

"That will be your father. Come to dinner. There will be no more talk of this matter."

He squared his shoulders and took her by the elbow. "Yes, ma'am."

The dining room door burst open with a mighty shove, and his father bolted into the room. His voice boomed and dishes rattled. "It's happened. Beauregard attacked Fort Sumter in Charleston!"

Peter's heart fell, and he cringed.

The horror had begun.

Chapter 14

Sweat beaded on Peter's brow. He loosened his collar and struggled for a breath of fresh air. Cigar smoke circled the room like a stagnant gray mist, and crawled across the Montgomery sitting room floor like a slow moving tobacco-reeking fog.

Obnoxious want-to-be politicians packed the room. Each had a smoke in one hand and a glass of fine Tennessee whiskey in the other. Peter weaved his way through the crowd, opened a window, and resisted the urge to jump out. Father's fundraiser for the Confederacy mirrored his personality. Loud and boastful. Why Father insisted on his presence was a mystery. Not knowing made him uncomfortable.

The rumble in the room silenced to a dull hum. Father strutted into the room. He held his hands up for silence and his voice roared.

"Friends, it is with great pride that we meet here tonight to honor our newly established Confederate States of American and her president, Jefferson Davis. I have an announcement to make concerning this matter." He motioned for Peter to step forward.

Peter tensed. What was Father up to? He walked, stiff and forced, across the floor. Dread tagged after him.

"As y'all know, my son, Peter, has recently graduated from West Point where, I'm proud to say, graduated in the top five of his class."

Peter bristled. Father had something big up his sleeve. He'd never voiced his approval of his accomplishments at the Point before. An uneasy feeling squirmed in his belly.

"I've been in contact with Mr. Davis, who has agreed that the South needs men the caliber of my son. Therefore, I'm proud to announce his commission into the Confederacy as a First Lieutenant in charge of a special cavalry unit supplied with thirty of the finest mounts in the Montgomery stables. He is to report to Richmond to assume his command and recruit his men."

Hell broke loose.

All cheered.

Whiskey poured.

Men pounded his back and pumped his hand.

The room spun.

Someone pushed a drink into his hand. He drained it in one gulp. His head pounded and his nerves danced.

"Well son? What say you?"

Father's act was an ambush. To refuse the commission would bring dishonor to the Montgomery name, and he wouldn't disgrace Mother. A fact Father knew only all too well. Once again Father had succeeded in finding a way to get rid of him. The urge to smack the smug look off Father's face burned down his arm to his wrist. He never hated the man more in his life.

"Fools."

Seeing the shock on Father's face felt almost as good as hitting him. Chaos broke loose, and Peter watched with immense satisfaction as Father tried in vain to regain order.

Peter's voice shook with anger, and he spit words hard as nails.

"The North will bury you. It was a sleeping dog. Do you think it cared about the South with its one-horse economy, backwoods politics, and government ruled by pretentious asses? Let it go and good riddance."

Peter drew a deep breath. Every eye trained on him.

"Your beloved Jefferson Davis gave his word that the South just wanted to be left alone and didn't wish war. Who are you to say different? With time and negotiation, the North would have turned over the U.S. forts, naval bases, and armories placed throughout the South to the Confederacy. But that wasn't good enough, and you continued to poke the beast with sticks of greed and power. Now, you've awakened the sleeping dog and turned it into a rabid, spitting animal. It will devour all of us and our land. The South and every good thing it stands for will be destroyed. Fools. All of you."

Silence blanketed the room. No one moved.

Fists clenched, he took a menacing step toward Father. Peter's eyelids pulled into slits, and fury hardened his soul. His voice, velvet smooth, but razor sharp, cut the quiet.

"And as for you, Father," he hissed. "You are worse than Judas. He willingly traded his soul for thirty bits of silver, but you stole mine for thirty pieces of horseflesh. May you burn in hell."

Peter turned on his heel and marched from the room.

Chapter 15

Peter leaned against the barn door and stared. Only days before, the stalls housed horses of every size, shape, and color. Father had wasted little time in sending the herd to Richmond. Most of the slaves had gone to help with the drive as well. Silence hung with the cobwebs waving from the beams and gave the barn an eerie, empty, ghost-like feel.

His lips hardened into a thin line. Since the fiasco in the sitting room three nights ago, he hadn't seen or spoken to Father. Rage had cooled to a smoldering ember of resentment, but the smallest event would fan his emotions into a blazing inferno. At the end of the week, he would ride to Virginia and assume command of a cavalry unit, not won for his West Point training or intellect, only bargained for in a bid for prestige and recognition. The commission was a joke, an insult to his hard work and intelligence. Father was wise to stay out of his way.

"Master Peter? Come quick. It's your mama!"

The look of fear on Amos's face turned his heart to stone. Side-by-side they stormed the house and burst into the parlor. His breath caught. Enveloped by her white skirts and lace petticoats, Mother lay on the polished floor like a wounded dove. Terrified, he knelt beside her and placed a trembling hand on her shoulder. "Mother?"

She gave a weak nod. "I'm all right, Peter."

"Amos. Help me get her to the sofa. Ruby. Get water."

They eased her onto the couch and winced at the bruise that defiled her bone-china face. Ruby pushed them to one side and placed a cold compress against the injured cheek.

"Just like old times, isn't it, my dear Ruby?"

"Yes, 'um. You hush now."

Panic washed over Peter. His face paled. "Sarah. Where's Sarah?"

"I just checked on her, suh. She's upstairs, asleep. She don't know nothin'."

"God bless you, Toby. What the hell happened?"

"It was him." Ruby spat. "Your daddy did this. They was arguin'. Over you. Over how he tricked you."

The anger that had simmered inside him came to a rolling boil, and he paced the floor, ready to explode. West Point trained him to handle many situations, but seeing Mother crumpled on the floor scared him to death. The more he paced, the more his blood bubbled until he became white hot with fury and lashed out. With a shout he grabbed the whiskey decanter from the desk and threw it at the wall. The stoppered container hit the window instead. Glass shattered. Cool wind whipped the curtains. A cold harshness blanketed the room like death. He wheeled.

"Toby, get Amos. Hitch up the carriage and the buckboard. Saddle my horse. Ruby, gather some extra clothes for Mother and Sarah and everything you can carry. Food, too."

No one moved.

A weak voice came from the couch. "Son? Have

you gone mad?"

"No, quite the opposite, Mother. I'm sending you and Sarah home, to Ravenswood, where you'll be safe. I should've done it long before now."

Toby drew him aside with concern in his eyes. "He'll follow her, suh. That's why she always stays."

A sinister smile pulled his lips, and a thin chill hung on the edge of his words. "Oh, Toby. I'm counting on it."

"Suh?"

"Toby, would you say Father is a well liked man in these parts?"

"No, suh, I would not."

"Then it would be fair to say he has enemies?"

"Yes, suh. A fair amount."

"You would agree then, that it could be dangerous for him to travel alone, especially on a long, deserted road?"

"I would."

"Therefore, it wouldn't surprise anyone to hear that he met with ill fortune on his way to Ravenswood?"

"No. It wouldn't."

His voice dropped and turned to steel. "No one need ever to fear Father again. Am I making myself clear?"

Peter watched understanding flicker in Toby's gray eyes. With a grim smile he raised them to lock with Peter's icy blue stare.

"Yes, suh. I believe I do."

Toby broke the glare and started for the stables.

Ruby darted from the room to collect blankets, clothes, and supplies, shouting over her shoulder. "Give us time. We'll fetch the carriage. Don't let her sway ya."

Worry creased his brow, and with anxious steps he returned to the settee and sat beside her. How small and fragile she looked, propped against the pillows, like a child's porcelain doll waiting for play. An elegant china doll with a broken face. Blue and purple stains circled her eye. The skin would be black by morning. He reached for her hand and pressed it to his heart. Why? Why did the innocent always suffer the sins of the guilty?

Her hand turned to caress his cheek. How typical. Even in her own pain she thought only to comfort his.

"Peter, it's only a bruise. It will heal with time."

He squeezed his eyes tight and fought to control the emotion that welled up inside of him. "*Your* scars may mend Mother, but no amount of time will cure mine. I've caused you so much pain, so much suffering."

She drew a deep breath, and he placed a finger gently on her lips to silence her. "No, Mother, not this time. There are no words you can say that will convince me I'm not to blame. Father was the brute that struck you, but I'm the one that gave him reason to." His voice broke.

"Nothing can change that, but I promise it will never happen again."

A winsome smile tugged the corners of his mouth. "It's time for you to stop the charade and to go home, Mother. Return to Grandfather and your precious Ravenswood. It's where you belong and where your heart has always been."

He squeezed her hand and glanced toward the bedrooms upstairs. "Live life without fear. Allow Sarah to be free, to grow up strong and confident. Encourage her independent nature so that she'll not fall victim to the will of others."

His gaze lowered, and he smoothed her hair back into place with a tender touch. "Every day I'll pray that the Union will spare you and your little corner of paradise from the death and destruction it will rain down upon the South."

The dull thud of horse's hooves and the jingle of reins and harnesses sounded through the broken window. In one fluid movement, he gathered her into his arms and carried her outside to the carriage. Then he returned for Sarah who curled next to Mother like a sleepy-eyed puppy.

"Toby? Is everything ready?"

"Yes, suh."

"Where's Amos?"

"Bringin' your horse as we speak, suh."

He hurried to meet the boy. "Are there any more horses left on this place?"

"Only one, suh. That strawberry roan mare. She's with foal."

"Take her. She and the baby are yours. Tell your pa to wait. I have one more thing to do."

He took the landing two steps at a time and burst into his room. His plan was bold. Did he have the courage to follow through with it? Mother's battered face flashed in his mind's eye. His teeth clenched. He pulled pen and paper from the desk drawer and wrote fast and furious.

He licked the last envelope shut and started down the stairs. As an afterthought, he returned to Sarah's room, grabbed the basket of kittens and Dixie, and raced back outside. Ruby grinned and placed the pets next to Sarah who slept a child's sleep, oblivious to the turmoil that surrounded her.

"Toby, I have three letters. One is for safe passage. It states that you and your family have my permission to travel with Mrs. Montgomery to her father's. I doubt you'll need it as Mother is with you. It's only a precaution. Give the second letter to Grandfather. It explains everything."

Peter hesitated and gazed into the darkness. Lives would change tonight because of his actions. Did he have the right to alter fate? Maybe it was his destiny to do so. Either way now wasn't the time to second guess himself.

"Toby, what you are about to do is a great sacrifice. I owe you a debt I fear I can never repay. This third letter is for you, Ruby, and Amos. Upon safe delivery of Mother and Sarah, Grandfather is to set you free."

Behind him Ruby gasped. Toby stood rooted to the ground, a stunned look written on his face. Tears leaked from his eyes and followed a blazed trail of laugh lines and crow's feet. He squeezed Peter's hand in affection and fumbled for words.

"Thank you, suh. But we will never leave Miss Virginia. We's been with her too long and love her like a daughter. You don't owe us nothin'. Your mama and her pappy kept me and my family together. Most wasn't that lucky. She never raised a hand against us or allowed anyone else to neither. And you? You always treated me and Ruby with respect. As equals. No, suh. We'll never leave your mama."

Tears burned on Peter's cheek. "Ah, Toby, don't

you see? That's the beauty of freedom. You can stay or leave. It's your choice. But for now, you must go. Be safe."

"But suh? What of this place? What should we do?"

"Grandfather will send for the remaining slaves and will take good care of them."

"What about the house?"

"Peter?"

He turned and walked to the side of the carriage. "Yes, Mother?"

"You are discussing this plantation as if it no longer exists. Your father might have something to say about that."

"Mother, this farm has been a gilded cage for you for many years. Father held you captive with his threats and lies. Pretend for a moment that he is no longer here. What would you do?"

Her face hardened and her voice rang out harsh and cold. "I'd burn it."

He kissed her for what he knew could be the last time, then turned to Toby. "Get in the wagon now and get out of here."

Toby climbed onto the seat and clucked to the team. Peter watched as the small caravan of wagons and horses disappeared into the mist.

He lit the torch.

Major snorted and danced as the flames shot higher and higher into the inky sky. Peter held him with a firm hand slid his Sharps carbine into the scabbard and stepped into the saddle.

He had a promise to keep.

Whisperings

Peter James Montgomery is the pin-up boy for the Confederate Army's recruiting poster. Strong, silent, impeccably dressed in razor-sharp uniform, he takes my breath away. Always the perfect Southern gentleman, polite almost to a fault, he is an expert at hiding his true feelings. Beneath his calm exterior, a deep darkness lurks. He is brooding and private and doesn't want to speak to me even though I sense he has much to tell.

I nag him to talk. Funny, isn't it—a mortal haunting a ghost? Peter, however, fails to see the humor. Perhaps it's a trust thing. I assure him I will stay true to his story. He tests my promise, giving me only tiny glimpses into his life. Satisfied, he begins to relax, and I struggle to write his words with the pride and passion he brings to them.

Perhaps it is only fitting that his turbulent silence breaks on a dark and stormy night (yes, I know how cliché that sounds) in early December. He hates his father. Interesting. "Why?"

"Mother," he answers.

Gallons of love pour over me when Peter talks about his mother. He is very much like her, sensitive and kind, good at deception. He adores the ground she walks on.

I type the scene between him and his mother on the veranda and am as surprised as she is to learn how philosophical Peter is. Respect begins to grow. He's patriotic. Loves his country as much as family. He's fearful war is emanate and afraid for the lives of the men he is yet to command.

Wow. This is good stuff. The storm outside intensifies. His story keeps pace. Then I type, "Does Father still beat you?" I about fall off my chair. No way did I see that coming.

My fingers fly across the keyboard. I hold my breath. What will he say next? The clock chimes midnight. My neck and back are killing me, but I keep typing. The dam has broken, and Peter is talking non-stop. No way will I shut him or my computer down.

I write the chapter and marvel at Peter's wit. Never would I equate his father's betrayal to that of Judas and Jesus.

The thunder booms outside and shakes the house. It's reminds me of a scene straight out of some Friday night horror movie. The storm builds to a crescendo and so does the chapter. When it dawns of me what is going to happen, I shout out loud.

"Oh, my God. He kills his father!"

I sit stunned, chill bumps race up my arms, and I stare at the words on the monitor. No wonder he is reluctant to tell his story.

"You must explain the reasons behind the action," he begs.

Even in death, Peter is searching for redemption.

Now, the promises are complete. Charlie and Jesse broke theirs. Peter kept his.

Three promises…two were broken; one should've been.

~R. H. Burkett

Chapter 16

The Horse Soldiers of Unit 547

"What's your name?"

"Charles Ely."

"Where you from?"

"Cougar Hollow, Virginia."

"Who's your next of kin?"

Charlie stared at the officer but didn't answer.

The lieutenant glanced up from the black record book and repeated the question. "Your next of kin?"

"Why do you need to know?"

Charlie heard the quick intake of breath from Tom who stood behind him. From the corner of his eye, he caught the surprised look on James's face.

The officer put down his pen, leaned back in his chair, and stared at Charlie with hawk eyes as sharp as the razor-edged creases of his uniform. Charlie held his look without flinching but couldn't help but wonder if he'd made a mistake by being so blunt.

The lieutenant pushed his hat back off his head and sighed. Sunlight bounced off his polished buttons and cast dull, brassy light across the table top. "I need a record of who to notify in case of death."

Charlie gaped.

James pushed past him. "That would be his ma, Clara Ely. My name is James Johnson. My pa is Albert, and my ma is Alice." He jerked his thumb toward Tom. "This is my friend, Tom Carpenter. His pa is Harvey."

"You got horses?"

"Yes sir! Charlie's ma got him a dandy and I…"

"Fine. Take yourselves and your horses a half mile down this road until you see a sign posted on a tree with the numbers 547 written on it. That's your unit. Stay put and wait for orders. You good with horses?"

"We know what end bites and what end kicks." Charlie broke into a sweat. Why did he say that?

James coughed and covered his mouth but not before Charlie saw the wide grin on his face, on the verge of laughing out loud. Tom ducked his head and focused on the ground as if seeing it for the first time.

The lieutenant studied him with a curious look. "Go on then. I need someone that knows more than that."

"I know just the man."

The voice came from the back of the line. Charlie paid little attention to the red-haired, freckled-faced kid that rushed by him as he hurried back toward the horses. All he wanted was to get away from the lieutenant before he said something else stupid.

James slapped him on the shoulder. "You made quite the impression back there, Charlie. Never heard you talk that way. What's wrong?"

They reached the hitching post and started to untie their horses when loud, boisterous laughter came from a white-washed building to their left. James tugged on Tom's sleeve and grinned. "Let's get a drink before we leave."

Charlie balked. Mother would disapprove.

"Aw, grow a backbone, Charlie," James whined.

"One drink ain't gonna hurt ya."

"He's right, Brown Eyes."

The husky, deep throated voice came from a woman who casually leaned her bare arms against the top of the saloon's swinging doors and smiled. Full, ruby red lips pouted. Dusky-rose blush set off her emerald eyes and raven hair. She winked at Charlie and stepped out onto the boardwalk.

"Come on in, Brown Eyes. The fun's just startin'." She took a few more steps, coming closer.

Charlie swallowed hard and tripped over Tom, whose feet had suddenly sprouted and grown roots, bringing them both to an abrupt stop. He struggled for a breath and managed to squeak out a dry, "No, thank you."

"Suit yourself, handsome. Your loss, not mine." With a toss of her head that sent her ebony curls flying, she turned and strolled slowly back into the barroom. Slim hips swayed with every step. The sweet scent of flowered perfume joined with her laughter and drifted past the batwing doors to linger and tease for a fleeting moment before fading into memory.

"Damn," Tom swore. "Was that a hussy?"

"Sure as shootin'." James laughed. "And she fancied you, Charlie, or should I say, Brown Eyes?"

Charlie dipped his head and felt the heat race up his neck and over his face.

"What makes you such an expert on fancy girls all of a sudden?" Tom asked as they mounted up.

"Well…I…I just heard about them, that's all."

Charlie didn't join the laughter, instead he spurred Red into a slow lope. His belly churned and sweat beaded his upper lip. The lieutenant's question unnerved him. Brought home the fact that death rode beside him. He tried to ignore the mental picture of Mother reading his death notice, but it trailed behind him as he rode toward his unit. The officer's words echoed in his ears.

"In case of death."

Chapter 17

"Specks, you're jumpin' like a frog on a hot rock. What's got you so riled up?"

The freckles on Specks' face danced. He tripped over his feet and gasped for breath. "Jesse! Come quick! There's a lieutenant that wants to see ya. Hurry! We got us a chance to ride."

"Ride? What ya talkin' about?"

"Horses! What else ya gonna ride?" He grabbed Jesse's arm and pulled. "I was standing in line when I overheard this officer say he needed a horse wrangler. I told him I knew just the feller. He wants to see ya. Come on, before he forgets who I am."

Jesse laughed. That wasn't possible.

The lieutenant raised his gaze from the leather record book and let his look travel over Jesse taking in his great size. "What's your name?"

"Jesse Brown." He nodded toward Specks and grinned. "That's my friend, Specks. Sometimes he's a little high strung."

"Hmm…noticed that. Tell me, Jess Brown. How do you know about horses?"

"I helped Pa raise and train the finest horses in Kentucky. We usually had around ten to twenty head to gentle out and break."

"I have thirty head of green broke ponies and a handful of men who joined the cavalry to ride instead of walk. Most of them only know what end of a horse eats and what end craps." He rubbed his chin. "Think you can help educate them?"

"Yes, sir." Jesse held his breath.

"Camp is halfway down this road. Unit 547. Report to a man called Gumpy. You can't miss him. He wears a beat-up hat with the brim pinned to the side and limps like a sore-footed mountain goat. Tell him I sent you. Pick out two horses for yourselves, but leave the dun alone. He's mine."

Gumpy wasn't hard to find and the bowlegged sergeant broke into a toothless grin when Jesse reported in.

"Hot damn!" Gumpy hopped from one leg to another. " 'Bout time the lieutenant sent me someone that knows manes from tails. I don't mind turning them hay burners over to ya one bit. No sireee, not one bit."

He spat a stream of tobacco and pointed at his mouth. "Think my front teeth fell out 'cause I'm old? Hell, no! Black witch of a mare kicked them out. Damn near split my head like a ripe melon." His lips stretched into a mischievous grin. "Come on. I'll introduce ya."

Jesse didn't believe his eyes. Thirty of the most striking horses he'd ever seen stood before him.

Gumpy fell into a spasm of laughter. "Had ya fooled, didn't I? Thought ya would find fire-breathin', ass-kickin', four-legged, devil monsters from hell, didn't yas'? I was just joshing. Best be gettin' acquainted with 'em. I weren't foolin' about turnin' them over to ya. I got other duties to tend to."

Specks watched the bow-legged man hobble away and shook his head. "I think that horse kicked more than that ol' coot's teeth out. He's half loco."

Jesse grinned and let out a low whistle. Heads raised and tails switched. "Specks, I think that officer was funnin' us too. These horses don't look green broke to me. I bet I could put a young'un on any one of 'em and he'd be as safe as if he was sittin' in a rockin' chair."

"Pick me out a good one, Jesse."

"Naw. You gotta choose your own."

Specks groaned. "Aw, Jesse. I don't ride so good. I need one of them rockin' chair ones."

Jesse started down the line and sighed. Specks was afraid, but then, when wasn't he? "Okay, walk with me, then. Maybe you'll get lucky and one will come to you. That's the best way. See that mare over yonder?"

"You talkin' about that one pawin' the ground? She's kinda pretty with that sleek, crow black coat, but that bowed-out nose ruins her looks."

"Yeah. Bet she's the one that tagged the ol' coot. Them Roman nosed horses are ornery and meaner than snake spit."

Specks jumped. Sharp teeth nipped his sleeve.

Jesse laughed. "It ain't nothin'. It's just Belle."

"Belle? Didn't your pa have a horse named Belle?"

Jesse swallowed hard. Even though the shy bay could pass as her double, he realized it wasn't Belle. But seeing how much she looked like the mare he remembered brought the name to mind and sparked a rush of memories. Unexpected tears welled in his eyes.

"Gosh Jesse. It's just like you said. She likes me. I'm claiming her, and I'm gonna call her Belle. That okay with you?"

"Sure." His voice turned husky. "Looks like she's a dandy."

"See any you fancy?"

Jesse shrugged and stared at the kaleidoscope of horses standing before him. Blacks. Bays. Chestnuts and sorrels. His gaze rested on a black piebald.

Specks followed his look. "You find one?"

"Yeah. Something about that one standing next to the lieutenant's gelding catches my eye."

"Looks like he's wearing a quilt of black and white patches. What ya goin' to call him?"

"Patch."

"That's a humdinger of a name. I'm hungry. Let's get back to camp and rustle up some grub."

"You go on. I'll catch up."

Jesse hung back on purpose. The sun slipped behind the horizon and vanished leaving only swirls of orange and purple as proof it was ever there. Day melted into dusk. Crickets tuned-up for their twilight songs. The evening was just like a hundred others, yet something was wrong. Maybe it was the excitement over working with horses again. What luck. Only days before he'd complained to Emmie... He frowned. It was Emmie who troubled him.

Not a day had gone by since he'd left home that he didn't think about her and guilt ate a hole in his gut. The last time he'd seen her she was sitting in the dirt, crying. He should've gone back and comforted her instead of turning away.

He hung his head and kicked at the ground. Maybe she'd been right when she called him and Pa cowards. He should've let her come with him. Consequences be damned. But what if he got killed, or even worse, captured? Who would watch over her then? What if she was the one that got shot or thrown into a Yankee prison camp? How could he live with himself?

The sound of a bugle broke his reverie. Must be suppertime. He walked toward camp and tried to push Emmie from his mind. She was better off at home. Wasn't she?

A lump rose in his throat. What if he never saw her again?

He scowled and shoved the thought of death deep into his soul. The notion settled next to the sting of Pa's abandonment and the hurt of Ma's rejection and waited for the fuse that would ignite its fury.

Chapter 18

Charlie shifted his weight from one foot to the other. A bunch of men swarmed around him, and he felt lost in the crowd. No one knew where to go or what to expect. Reminded him of the first day of school when shy, uncertain groups of children waited for their teacher to tell them what to do. A tall, freckled-faced kid bumped his shoulder.

"Sorry partner." Specks offered his hand. "My name's Specks, from Kentucky."

Charlie shook with him. "I'm Charles Ely, from Virginia." He nodded to his right. "These are my friends, Tom Carpenter and James Johnson."

"Howdy. Y'all as hungry as me? I swear my stomach thinks my throat's been cut."

Tom laughed. "Smells like hushpuppies. Hope so. Nothin' better than fried cornbread."

"I remember you," James said. "You were in line behind us. You the feller that knows horses?"

"Naw, that's my friend, Jesse." Specks searched the crowd. "Here he comes now. Hey, Jesse! Over here! This here is Charlie, Tom, and James. They hail from Virginia."

Jesse wiped his hand on his pant leg and swallowed Charlie's hand in his. "Specks been talkin' your ear off?"

Charlie laughed. "Is that his real name?"

Specks jumped in. "Noooo. It ain't. My given name is God-awful. Hate it. Jesse nicknamed me Specks 'cause of my freckles, which by the way are God-awful. Hate them too."

"I ain't never heard of nobody not likin' their name before. What is it?" Tom asked.

"Come and get it!"

Specks ignored the question and headed for the front of the chow line.

Jesse lowered his voice and whispered, "It's Elmer."

"Elmer? That ain't a bad name," Tom replied. "My pa had a mule named Elmer."

Jesse grinned. "Your pa and every damn farmer in Kentucky. That's why he hates it."

Charlie relaxed and joined in the laughter. He liked Specks and Jesse, even though they were different as night and day. Specks reminded him of a tail wagging, speckled pup while Jesse seemed down to earth and solid as an ox.

Specks raced back to the group. His ruddy complexion had faded to the color of wheat paste. He gasped. "Good God."

Jesse grabbed him by the arm. "What's wrong? You look like you've seen a ghost."

"He ain't got no leg!"

"Who ain't?"

"The cook."

They eased to the front of the line and stared in disbelief. A man wearing a grease-stained apron leaned on a rough carved wooden crutch. His left pant leg was tied up in a dangling knot at the knee, and he jumped back and forth.

"See?" Specks gaped. "I told ya. He's a cripple."

Charlie watched Jesse's face turn a candied-apple red.

He glared at Specks. "Shhh! Bet he knows. Just act like nothin's wrong."

Specks rolled his eyes. "Well, I ain't never seen a man with half a leg before. Goin'a be damn hard not to notice."

Charlie bit his lip to keep from laughing. If the cook heard or noticed their stares, he chose to ignore them. They sat in a semi-circle and ate heaping plates of beans and hushpuppies. He glanced at Tom, and James shook his head. This had been quite a day, and wasn't over yet.

A shadow fell over them. The circle hushed.

"My name is Lieutenant Peter James Montgomery. Pay attention. Get it right. Won't be saying it again. Your unit is 547. Remember that. Sergeant Wendell Gump, Gumpy, is second-in-command. Your cook's name is Jumper. That's all the introductions I'm making. Get to know one another on your own time. A word to the wise. Don't get used to having hot meals or tents. They're a temporary luxury. Horses will be assigned tomorrow for any boys that didn't bring their own." A slight grin crossed his face.

"Trust me, you'll get to know every bob of their head, roll of their eyes, and switch of their tails before this is over with. That's all."

Thunder rumbled in the distance and the weak, lazy breeze grew in strength. One-by-one, men broke from the circle to hurry to their tents before the storm hit.

Charlie lay on his cot and listened to the first sprinkles of rain tap on the canvas. The whine of a harmonica drifted through the dark. For the first time since leaving home, he let his thoughts roam free. Mother's face came to him, and he gulped back a sob. She would be washing the supper dishes along about now. Maybe she would sit by the fire and knit before going to bed, or read. She liked books, especially the ones about far-away places like London or Rome. His heart knotted tighter. Sure did miss her.

A rustling noise came from the corner, and he eased himself onto his elbows. Tom sat on the edge of his bed and stared at this pocket watch. Looking over at Charlie, he mumbled, "Just checkin' the time. Seems later than what it is."

Charlie nodded but knew Tom's mind was on other things. It was too dark to see the watch's face. Thoughts of home must be wandering in Tom's mind.

James let out a yell. "Lines!"

Charlie caught Tom's confused look. "You dreamin' over there, Jimboy?"

"What? Me? No. It just come to me. This army does everything in lines. We rode here in a line, we signed-up in a line, our horses are tied to a line, we lined up for supper, and our tents are pitched in a line."

Charlie chuckled. "What's your point?"

"We'll never get lost."

"How ya figure that?"

"We'll never ride in circles. We'll always go forward and straight."

Laughter filled the tent and thoughts of home ran out the door. Charlie waited for sleep and was almost at the edge of dropping off when James, once again, destroyed the silence.

"Lilly Rose."

He leaned up and glanced at Tom. "Who?"

"Lilly Rose."

"Who's that?"

"The saloon girl I asked to marry me."

Chapter 19

James grinned to himself, watching Charlie and Tom sit up and swing their feet to the ground. He purposely remained silent, letting their curiosity build. The rotten-egg smell of a lit match tickled his nose, and seconds later the yellow glow from the lantern cast giant-sized shadows of them. They dragged their cots closer to his. Their stares bored through him.

"You been holding out on us," Tom said. "Ever since we was kids we told each other everything. Took a blood-brother oath on it. Sealed it with spit. Why you just now telling us this?"

"I couldn't. You know Ma. If she'd found out I was in love with a saloon girl, she'd hog-tie me and never let me out of the house."

"Whoa! Just a minute!" Charlie said. "Love? Did you say love?"

James nodded and a hangdog grin crossed his face. "Yeah. We're going to get married when I come back from the war."

Minutes passed.

James stared at the ground.

Tom exploded. "Well? What ya waiting on? Your mama ain't here now. You going to tell us?"

"Remember a few months back when I delivered some of our old furniture to a hotel in the next town?"

"I remember," Charlie said. "Is that when you met

her?"

"Yeah. When the man at the hotel paid me for the chairs, he threw in a few dimes more, said he was grateful I saved him a trip. He winked and told me not to spend it all on women and whiskey at the saloon down the street."

"Hell." Tom snorted. "He had to know that's the first place you'd go."

"Course he did. I weren't in any hurry to go home. It was the first time Pa let me go anywhere without him. I wanted to make the most of it."

"What about the girl?" Charlie nudged.

"Hold your horses." James grinned. He enjoyed being the center of attention and intended to make the most of it. "I heard music, so I followed the sound and stopped in front of the One-Eyed Horse saloon. Ma calls saloons, 'dens of iniquity,' so I just leaned on the swinging doors and looked around before going in."

Tom shot Charlie a puzzled look. "What does *iniquity* mean?"

"Sin."

"Damn." He turned back to James. "Did you see any of that iniquity?"

"I ain't for sure what sin is supposed to look like. But that place was lit up like the Fourth of July. A man with a bowler hat banged on an old piano and music bounced off the walls. Everyone hooted and hollered. So I strutted in, bellied up to the bar, and ordered me a beer."

"What'd it taste like?"

"Bitter. I drank it but didn't like it much. I got a snort of whiskey next."

"You're joshing."

"It had a sweet, tangy taste. Went down smooth, but kicked like a mule."

"What about the girl?"

"There was three of them."

"God Almighty. Three?" Tom's eyes bugged from his head.

"Yep. They wore frilly red dresses with bunches of feathers glued to them. When they danced and kicked up their heels, you could see their black petticoats."

"Lace petticoats? This is too much." Tom groaned.

"Were the girls pretty?" Charlie asked.

"They'd be prettier if they'd washed some of that war paint off they was wearing. One of them had scarlet hair. Red as a sun ripe tomato. She kept running her hands up my arm and called me honey. Made me hot and itchy. The taller one had coal black hair that coiled around her head like a lariat on a saddle. I wanted to reach out and touch it so bad, I could've spit. Her black eyes matched her hair, and thick lashes almost hid them. Kinda like yours, Charlie. Her skin was a soft, buckskin color."

"I'm guessing the third one was Lilly. What'd she look like?"

James stilled, and his mind wandered back to that far away place. "She had an angel face, small and heart-shaped. Silky, wheat spun hair flowed past her shoulders like a waterfall of honeycomb. Kinda shy. And short. Only came to my shoulder. Not any bigger round than a dogwood sapling. Robin-egg-blue eyes danced and sparkled like stars reflecting on water. We stood there and stared at one another. Had the feeling I'd known her all my life. She took my breath away."

Silence filled the tent for several moments, no

sounds but Tom's pocket watch ticking off the seconds. The pitch was like small pebbles ricocheting off the canvas. James emerged from his dream-like state and blinked at the wonder and surprise in Charlie's and Tom's expressions. "What ya gawkin' at?"

Charlie cleared his throat. "Never heard you talk that way before. Didn't know you could be so romantic."

"What happened next?"

"The brassy redhead wanted me to buy drinks. I didn't have any idea what to get, so I bought three sarsaparillas. Well, ol' Scarlet damn near busted a gut laughing. She grabbed the dark-haired gal and told Lilly that the tenderfoot was all hers. I asked Lilly if I done something wrong. Told her I got sarsaparilla instead of beer 'cause I didn't know what ladies drank."

"What did she say?"

"Her eyes filled with tears, and I could've kicked myself for doing something so stupid and bad. Told her I was sorry. Didn't mean to insult anyone or do anything wrong." He paused and shook his head. "She just smiled at me through those blue eyes swimming in water, and said I didn't do nothing wrong. In fact, I'd done everything just right."

Tom placed his hands on his knees, locked his elbows, and leaned forward. "Ain't that just like a woman? They sure do like to confuse a fella."

Charlie and James roared with laugher. "Like you'd know," James teased.

"What happened next?"

"She took my hand and asked me to go upstairs to her room."

Tom fell off the bed.

Charlie gaped, open mouthed. "You shooting square, or pulling our legs?"

"I'm square."

Both Charlie and Tom asked, "Did ya go?"

"I wanted to, but..." He squirmed. "I...I was scared." He glanced at Charlie and took a deep breath. "You know. I ain't never been with a woman."

Tom and Charlie exchanged understanding nods.

"I was too embarrassed to tell her that, but she seemed to know. Then she said something I'll never forget."

"What?"

"She told me never to judge a book by its cover."

"What the hell did that mean?"

"She said just 'cause she worked in a dance hall it didn't mean she was for hire. Said she wasn't like Scarlet. When she took a man to bed, it was 'cause she wanted to, and money had nothing to do with it."

Tom scoffed. "And you believed her? A painted-up, petticoat-showin' hussie?"

Charlie pushed back from James and braced for the explosion.

With cat-like speed James lunged and grabbed Tom by the front of his shirt. "Don't ever call her that again," he hissed between clenched teeth.

"*You* called her that."

"That was before I knew her." James tightened his grip. "There are times when a woman's gotta do what she has to, same as a man. She's alone, got no man to care for her, so she sings and dances in a saloon. But that's all she does. Understand?"

"I didn't mean nothin' by it." Tom lowered his gaze. "Sometimes I wonder if I'll ever find a girl that will love me. I ain't got nothin' to offer one. I smell like horse poop and hay all the time. Ain't got two bits to my name. Guess I'm just jealous."

James dropped his hands. Tom's heart-felt confession surprised him and cooled his anger. He walked to the door of the tent and flipped back the canvas. Sweet rain flavored breeze swept through and cleared the air. Tom coughed.

"Sorry, James. It won't happen again. Tell us more about Lilly."

"Did you ever go upstairs with her?" Charlie asked.

"Sure did. Her room was a little slice of heaven. Heavy looking things she called tapestry hung on the walls and blocked the noise from downstairs. A blood-red rug covered the floor. Bright colored curtains wrapped around her windows like bows on Christmas packages. Ever'where I looked there were pretty things. She had rosy-pink dishes in every nook and cranny." He paused and glanced at Charlie.

"And books. She had books everywhere. Said she loved to read 'cause she could escape to far off places and be anyone she wanted to. In the corner by the window, she had a big rocking chair and a gray and white cat was curled in its cushion. A settee smothered with pillows was in the middle of the room. Then, of course, there was the bed."

"Did she take you over to it?"

"No. We nestled on the settee and talked. She curled around me like that cat in the rocker. I can't explain it. I never felt so relaxed in all my life."

"Talked? That's all?"

"Yep." James winked. "For the first night."

"The first night? How many nights were you

there?"

"Every night for six months. I'd wait till Ma and Pa went to bed. Then I high-tailed it to town."

"Well…did you continue to just talk?" Tom asked.

"No. And that's all I'm saying about that."

"When did you ask her to marry you?"

"I told her I was going to join the war. She didn't try to talk me out of it. Said that a man had to do what he thought was right. I told her I loved her from the moment I first saw her. She said she fell in love with me when I bought a sarsaparilla for a lady. That's when I asked her." He dropped his head and shrugged his shoulders. "Guess y'all think that's silly, and I'm acting like a love-sick pup."

"No." Charlie smiled. "I think it's nice to have someone that believes in you."

"Yeah, me too," Tom said.

"Hope this war gets over soon," James said. "Somehow I ain't as excited about it as I first was." He blew out the lantern and dark silence surrounded them.

Just before dozing off, Charlie chuckled. "But you *are* a love-sick pup."

James closed his eyes and listened to the brotherly laughter that spilled out into the night.

Whisperings

Charlie knows the importance of confirmation, those tiny pieces of physical proof that give credence to what he tells me and spurs me forward.

These valuable tidbits of verifications come from many directions and sources. All that is required of me is an open and alert mind.

A picture frame, decorated with a gun belt and holster, hangs in my living room, a housewarming gift. "Don't have any idea why I bought this for you," a close friend says, "but something told me it was important for you to have." I'd just finished the chapter where Clara gives Charlie his father's gun, gun belt, and holster.

Coincidence or truth?

Another friend with shoulder-length, black hair swears someone is pulling her curly locks. A few weeks before I'd written the chapter on Lilly Rose where James says, "One girl had coal black hair that coiled around her head like a lariat on a saddle. I wanted to reach out and touch it so bad, I could've spit."

Coincidence or truth?

In my kitchen I have a lighted china hutch that is home to Mama's wedding china and Grandma's antique dishes. Once a year I hand wash every piece and return them to their designated spot. This year an overwhelming urge compels me to place the rose-colored dishes in the forefront instead of in back. Their pink glow is beautiful in the soft light. Lilly Rose has "rosy-pink dishes in every nook and cranny."

Coincidence or truth?

Horses play such an important role in the story, especially Red. I struggle to capture the essence of each. My Secret Santa at work gives me a wall calendar of horses. I flip it open and there, in all their glory, stands Crow, Belle, Major, and Patches. I tear out the pages, frame the images, and hang them in my office above my computer. A 4'x2-1/2' framed picture of the exact image of Red hangs on one of my living room walls, a birthday gift from my brother.

Coincidence or truth?

Skeptics argue.

Others laugh.

Many wonder.

The enlightened believe.

I know.

Truth is stranger than fiction.

~R. H. Burkett

Chapter 20

Peter gazed into the lantern's glow. Behind him the sound of laughter floated on the wind, but he sat barely aware of its presence. The flickering flame pulled him away from reality into shadowed memories that haunted both his sleeping and waking hours. Killing Father. Too easy. One shot. A quick squeeze of the trigger solved everything. Almost. Heaviness settled on his shoulders. Remorse? Guilt? Neither. Regret? Only for not doing it sooner. What kind of man commits cold-blooded murder and feels nothing? An evil one?

He shook free from the all-too-familiar feeling of melancholy, reached toward his coat hanging on a chair, and fumbled in his pocket for pipe and tobacco. The lieutenant's bars on the jacket's collar flashed in the lantern's light and caught his stare. They mocked him with their silent symbolism.

A cynical smile curled his lips. Now he understood. This command was his penance. To answer for the death of one, he must atone by being responsible for the lives of many. This unit comprised of boys trapped between adolescence and manhood—between hay and grass—was his atonement.

A shadow flashed in the corner of his eye. "Lieutenant? You there?"

"Sergeant? Is there a problem?"

"No sir. Thought you could use some coffee."

He smelled the steaming cup and wrinkled his nose. "There's more than coffee in here."

"Jumper said you take a snort 'round about this time."

Peter took a sip and waited for the sting of the bumblebee drink to stop the haunting. Blessed whiskey. If he drank enough, Father's face would disappear.

Laughter reached him. "Listen to them, Gump. They sound like Sunday School boys on a church picnic."

"Yep, that they do." He squatted on his heels. "Young bunch of pups for sure. Doubt some of them even shave yet."

"Half of them will be killed in our first fight. It's enough to make a man sick."

"Or drive him to drink," Gumpy said.

Peter cocked an eyebrow. "It's my responsibility to stop that from happening."

"*Yours?*" Gumpy stood and scratched his whiskered chin. "You ain't God. This is war. Getting kilt could happen to any one of us. Don't fret over what you can't control."

"I have to."

Peter's outburst caused Gumpy to study him closely. He returned the man's burning stare without flinching, but his gut twisted. "What I mean is a commanding officer must try."

"How ya figure on doing that?"

"Training. Tomorrow we start. Marksmanship. Horsemanship. Tactics. Hand-to-hand. Sword…"

"Peter. Stop."

Peter scowled. He didn't know what shocked him most, the sound of his first name or the strict demanding tone that delivered it.

"This ain't West Point. Half these boys ain't never seen a rifle. We ain't got time to bottle feed them. *Your* duty is to get them battle-ready in the shortest time possible." He placed a knotted hand on Peter's shoulder. "Me and Jump been soldiers for a long time. We ain't never seen an officer care about his men as much as you. Take those horses for example. They's private stock. Could be from your own stables. Each man's got two pairs of pants, shirts, a warm jacket, and two blankets. The Confederacy didn't issue all that. If'n I was a bettin' man, and I am, I'd say you had something to do with that too. Why?"

Gumpy clicked his tongue. "A man don't drink as much as you lessen' he's got a mighty powerful reason. Ain't none of my business what demons chase ya. But you can only do so much. Ya can't save them all. Leave the living and dying up to God."

"I'll take your advice under consideration." Peter's cold tone signaled the end of the conversation. "Tell Jumper thanks for the coffee and keep plenty on hand."

"Sure thing." Gumpy turned to leave.

"Sergeant?"

"Yes, sir?"

"Don't ever call me Peter again."

Gumpy gave a half salute and nodded. "Yes, sir."

Peter returned to his seat by the lantern, tapped tobacco into his pipe, and drew a deep breath. The smooth smell of vanilla mixed with the spring rain and floated lazily on the night air. The tobacco settled him. More likely, it was the whiskey. His brow furrowed in deep thought.

The advice given by his salty sergeant was sound,

but the words didn't matter. The blood of every soldier in this unit was on his hands and conscience. He was guilty of murder.

No sin would go unpunished.

Chapter 21

"Watch out for her, John. She's a witch with four legs and a tail."

Standing around the makeshift corral of fresh-hewn tree limbs, everyone laughed and yelled encouragement. They'd waited all day for this match up. Jesse's brow furrowed. No one volunteered to ride the ill-tempered mare, Crow. He had to make the decision. Little Luke Harrison—Shorty—wanted her. But Jesse dismissed him. They'd argued about it all afternoon until Jesse had enough.

"Luke, Crow is stubborn, big, and mean. No offense, but she needs a larger man with stronger hands than you. You're the size of a matchstick. She'd break you in half."

Luke's temper was as short as his legs, and he fired back. "Just 'cause I'm not the size of a grizzly bear, don't mean I can't ride. You're judging me on looks, and ain't willing to give me a chance to prove myself."

"I said, no. I ain't gonna have a man get killed for the sake of his pride. Take the Chestnut with the white socks and go on."

Frustrated and angry, Luke stomped away muttering under his breath and shaking his head like an old man, but Jesse ignored him. He'd made up his mind. John McGraw would get Crow.

Well over six feet, with hands the size of ham

hocks, John oughta be able to control the roman-nosed mare without much trouble. However, Jesse's jaw tightened when Crow pinned her ears back and nipped at John when he reached for the reins. Behind him, he heard Luke chuckle.

The cantankerous mare eyed the big man with suspicion. For each step John took toward her, she'd back-up two. Sidestepping in a circle, she stopped him from reaching her until he jerked the reins hard, and she threw her head in protest. John moved quick, grabbed a hunk of mane, and plopped his beefy butt into the saddle. A grunt of surprise rose from deep in her belly, and she crow-hopped for a few feet, then balked.

Confident he had mastered the mare, John spurred her flanks. Crow exploded like a swollen can of rotten beans. She dipped her head, bowed her back, and bucked like a jack rabbit. The reins snapped in half, and John pitched forward in the saddle. Whack! His chin hit the horn, and he lost a stirrup. A collective groan rose from the group of men.

"He's buzzard bait now." Specks laughed and slapped his knee.

Taking advantage in the shift of weight, the inky mare reared and flung her head like a rainbow trout on a line. John somersaulted over the cantle of the scarred Texas rig, hit the sun-baked ground, and bounced. Jesse and the rest of the men ran to his aid, all except Luke. Doubled over in laugher the small man stayed his ground.

When two teeth fell out of John's bloody mouth into Gumpy's hand the leathery sergeant yelled, "Told ya that black is meaner than cougar piss."

Crow pawed the ground. Her onyx mane and tail

whipped in the wind, giving her a wild, witchy look. Jesse stood and started toward her, then hesitated when her pin ears flew backward. Luke walked past him.

"She'll kill you!" Jesse said and grabbed the man's arm.

"Naw," Luke said with a grin and shook off Jesse's hand. "She's my kind of woman."

"Let me at least ear her down while you get a new bridle on her."

Luke reached up and twisted Jesse's ear.

"Ow! You sawed-off son-of-a bitch! Whatcha do that for?"

"Hurts, don't it? She wouldn't like it neither. I'll loop a lead rope around her neck."

Maybe Luke made a good point.

With slow, deliberate steps Luke approached the skittish mare. She shook her head and snorted inquisitively at the lead rope in Luke's outstretched hand but stood her ground. In a soothing, sing-song voice he reached around her blue-black shoulder glistening with sweat, and tied off the lead rope.

He stepped up into the stirrup.

Jesse took in a sharp breath.

Still moving slow and talking soft, Luke eased into the saddle. He made no move for a few minutes, then with a slight nudge of his slick heel, he cued the mare forward.

Jesse's jaw dropped. How did Luke charm Crow into submission?

A smug grin spread across Luke's face when he rode past Jesse, then he turned back. Leaning forward on the saddle horn, he stared Jesse square in the eye.

"Never knew a woman, two-legged or four, that

didn't favor a gentle touch and a kind word to a hard, demanding one."

A slow smile broke Jesse's face. He'd underestimated Luke. Judged him unfairly. Sometimes determination, gumption, and brains outweighed brut strength. This was a lesson he'd not forget.

He turned to Big John who had managed to sit up but still looked dazed and dizzy.

"You ride the Chestnut from here on out."

John just fell over backwards with a loud groan.

The afternoon passed quickly. The sun cast long shadows on the ground, and the air turned cool. The low rumble of thunder sounded in the distance. Jesse stared at the sky. Blue and clear. No rain clouds in sight. Target practice had ended for the day, and Jesse walked to his tent, still searching the sky for rain. He glanced over at Specks sitting on a scared tree stump with his rifle and cleaning rag in hand.

"I swear I hear thunder," Jesse said. "But there ain't a cloud in the sky."

"I don't hear nothin'," Specks said and continued to rub the Springfield's barrel.

"I'm bored," Jesse said leaning on his musket. "What good is all this training if we never get a chance to use it?"

"Aw, I don't mind it that much," Specks said. "Them straw targets don't shoot back."

"Just the same, I'm tired of waiting around. I want some action."

"Yeah, well…be careful what you wish for."

The sound of thunder roared, and the ground shook. Specks frowned and put his rifle down. "Did ya hear it this time?" Jesse asked.

"Yeah, but it ain't thunder. Look!"

Two men on horseback raced toward them. Jumping back from the charging horses, Jesse felt the heat from their mounts' bodies and smelled the sour sweat on their lathered shoulders. The lead horse stumbled in exhaustion. Pulling sharply on the reins, the pasty-faced soldier in the saddle screamed at Jesse. "You got a sawbones in this outfit?"

"Yeah, but…"

"Get him and hurry!"

"I'll go!" Specks yelled and took off in a dead run.

The second horse stopped inches from Jesse's back, and its rider slumped forward onto its neck. Jesse eased him to ground and gasped as blood covered his hands and arms.

By this time camp looked like a stomped-on anthill. Men poured out of their tents, gathered in small groups, milling around and yelling. Specks ran forward with the lieutenant. Jumper hobbled and limped behind them, carrying a black bag.

"That's your doctor?" the first rider cried. "A worn-out, half-legged cripple?"

"I tried tellin' ya," Jesse said.

The lieutenant took the rider by the hand and steered him away from the group. "I'm Lieutenant Montgomery. What's this all about?"

"Private Reynolds, sir," the boy said and gave a hasty salute. "We was ambushed about ten miles from here. That man on the ground is Corporal Williams. Sergeant Jackson is bringing the rest of the wounded in on wagons."

Jesse watched surprise and concern flash across the lieutenant's face. "I didn't think the enemy was this close."

"No, sir. Neither did we. Think it was a stray patrol, caught us off guard."

The lieutenant wheeled. "Gump, post guards!" He turned back to the boy. "How many is your sergeant bringing?"

"Maybe ten. Don't rightly know. Them blue bastards were on us like ducks on June bugs. Sarge told me and Williams to ride ahead and find a doctor. I didn't know the corporal was that bad shot." He turned and walked back to Jumper. "Is he gonna make it?"

"Gut shot. Doubt it," Jumper said.

"Here they come!" Jesse yelled.

Two wagons pulled by wild eyed, sweat drenched horses wheeled into camp.

"Brown, get some men and get the wounded out of those wagons," the lieutenant yelled. "Put them in the cook tent for now."

Jesse grabbed Specks and yelled at Charlie. "Come, on! Hurry!" Tom and James ran beside them. Specks reached the wagon first and stopped dead in his tracks. The stench of blood and the buzzing of flies made him retch. Jesse slapped him on the back.

"Puke later."

Charlie crawled into the wagon and began helping the soldiers with less serious wounds.

Tom and James carried the more critical to the tent. Specks and Jesse followed. In one swipe of his arm, Gumpy cleared the tables. Jumper said nothing as he hobbled from one soldier to another, throwing buckets of water on the tables to wash off the blood between patients.

Specks stood spellbound, face pale, tears in his

eyes, watching soldiers scream and moan with pain.

"Come on, Specks," Jesse said. "We've done all we can. Help me tend to their horses."

The easy, laid back pace of camp turned into chaos and panic. Rumors of the Yankees being only a stone's throw away grew until the stray patrol became a full battalion marching to attack. Hours passed without incident and only then did everyone calm down. Guards, however, walked the parameter, and weapons were kept at close range.

Tired and hungry, Jesse dropped to the grass and pulled makings from his pocket. He shook tobacco onto a paper and rolled the cigarette into a tight stick and glanced at Specks from the corner of his eye. "If ya got somethin' stuck in your craw, spit it out."

"Here," Jesse said. "Have a smoke."

Specks reached for the cigarette and nodded at Charlie when he walked up on them.

"Hey, Charlie," Jesse said. "Want a smoke?"

Charlie shook his head and sank to the ground across from Jesse and Specks forming a triangle shape in the grass. "No thanks. Just came from the cook tent. Corporal Williams died."

"God damn it to Hell," Specks said.

"It ain't fair." He pulled in a long drag from the cigarette and watched the tip glow red and spit orange sparks.

"Take it easy, Specks," Jesse said. "This is war. Men die in battle."

"It weren't no battle," Specks snapped. "It was just a skirmish. Can you imagine what a real fight is gonna be like?"

When Charlie and Jesse didn't answer, he

continued. "I don't think we know what we're in for, and I'm scared. I don't want to be a coward, but I don't know if I can do this."

Jesse was quiet. The same thought crossed his mind more than once, but unlike Specks, he didn't dwell on it. Needless worry was a waste.

Specks stubbed his cigarette into the ground and watched the smoke coil around his boot like a lazy, gray snake. He glanced at Jesse then at Charlie.

"Have y'all ever wondered what it's like to die?"

Chapter 22

A queasy feeling stirred in the pit of Charlie's belly. He'd come to terms with Pa's death long ago, but Specks' question resurrected the emotions. Sorrow and confusion had overwhelmed him for years, but Mother accepted it and hardly grieved at all. Why?

"Because," she'd explained, "the soul never dies. Pa lives on in another world that people can't see."

Even though too young to completely understand, he never questioned her belief. Mother never lied. Besides, he drew comfort from knowing that, somewhere, Pa was alive. The older he got, however, the more he warmed to the notion. Often he spoke to Pa as if he were standing beside him. Sometimes he could feel his presence guiding and protecting him. Mother understood, but he learned the hard way that very few others shared their ideas of life after death.

"You're loco," James had said.

"Quit scaring me, Charlie." Tom's face had turned white. "That there is devil talk."

If his blood brothers didn't believe him, no one would, so he locked his feelings deep inside and spoke only to Mother about his faith. No, dying didn't scare him, but talking about it did. Now, Specks threatened to open a Pandora's Box of emotions and ideas that he wasn't sure he wanted to share.

"Charlie, your face is the color of warmed-over

milk toast. Did I say something wrong?"

"No, Specks, you just made some rusted memories jump to mind. After Pa died, Mother and I talked a lot about death."

"Did you wonder why God took him?" Specks asked.

"Yeah."

"Did your mama help make sense of it?"

"Enough."

"Then you was lucky. I wondered the same thing when my Mama died, but I didn't have no one I could talk to about it, except Jesse."

"And I weren't much help," Jesse said. "All I could tell him was that she went to heaven."

Specks squirmed and glanced over his shoulder, making Charlie wonder what made him so nervous. "Specks? What's got you so jumpy? The lieutenant said that Yankee patrol is long gone."

"I'm just makin' sure we can talk honest without someone interrupting us."

"Honest about what?" Jesse asked.

"Heaven and Hell." Specks drew in a deep breath. "I ain't sure I believe in them."

Jesse's right eyebrow arched, giving him a questioning look.

"I don't want to talk again' God or commit any sin, but the whole thing don't make sense to me."

"I don't think it's a sin, Specks," Charlie said. "Ever since the beginning of time, people have wondered what happens after they die. It's natural to talk about it. Go ahead."

"I'm with Charlie," Jesse said and started rolling another cigarette. "What's on your mind?"

"Back home, Preacher Harris yelled and screamed about the pits of Hell, stinkin' and burnin' with fire, ruled by a demon with a cloven hoof and pointed tail. But folks have dug some mighty deep wells, and they ain't never smelled or seen such a thing. He said Heaven had roads of gold, winged angels, and a saint guarding its gate. If God rules Heaven, why would someone have to guard it?"

Charlie couldn't help but smile. He'd misjudged Specks. At first glance, the lanky redhead appeared to be just a happy-go-lucky, naïve kid with little education. But the more he listened, the more he realized Specks was a deep thinker with a good head on his shoulders. Mother would like him. The kind of boy she loved to teach. No telling where this conversation was headed or would wind up.

"In other words," Jesse said. "When you're dead, you're dead."

"Well, that's the rub," Specks said. "Don't ya think that's a waste? I mean, why would God take the time to make all of us, if there weren't more than just livin' a few years, then nothing? What do you think, Charlie?"

"I think, you think, you're going to die."

A sarcastic snort came from Specks, and he rolled his eyes. "Seein' how we're in the middle of a war, gettin' ready to go into battle, I'd have to say, yeah, the thought's crossed my mind a few hundred times."

"And you're afraid."

"Hell's bells, Charlie! Course I am. Ain't you?"

A tingle raced up Charlie's spine. *Choose your words carefully, Charlie boy, or you may regret it.*

"I don't want to die, that's for sure, but I'm not afraid to."

"Why?" Jesse asked.

The tingle turned into an icy chill. The moment of truth hovered. He shifted in the grass and pulled at the dandelions waving in the evening breeze. Big John lumbered past, and Charlie waited until the clumsy ox was out of earshot, then took in a long breath.

"I think we live on, but not necessarily in this body."

The silence was deafening.

Charlie looked at first one friend, then another. Jesse sucked on his cigarette like he was going to swallow it.

Color ran from Specks' face. "You mean, like a ghost?" he squeaked and pulled his rifle closer.

Nice going, Charlie boy. You just ripped the hinges right off that box of secrets.

Darkness fell like a stone and surrounded them. Pinpricks of campfires dotted the inky bivouac, and the smell of burning wood drifted through the air. Behind them a screech owl let out a blood-curdling scream, and Specks leaped from the ground, rifle in hand. His gaze darted from one direction to the next.

"Maybe we should light a lantern," Charlie said, and tried to hide his grin. "Listen, we should stop all this talk. It's got Specks spooked, and y'all think I'm crazy."

"Shoot, Charlie. We thought that long ago," Specks said with a nervous laugh. "I ain't scared of the dark, neither, but I think a lantern would be a good idea. Wouldn't want Big John to stumble over us if he comes back."

"I'll get one from the tent," Jesse said with a chuckle.

Fog moved in on silent cat paws. Specks sat close to Charlie and pulled his collar up around his neck and ears. A chill rode the wind along with the smell of damp grass. Charlie heard Specks' quick intake of breath as two lights bobbed toward them, then a sigh of relief when Jesse's figure came into sight.

"I brought two," Jesse said and handed a light to Specks. Sitting down opposite them, he placed the second lantern beside him. The flame danced and cast an eerie glow against their faces and the backdrop of black sky and twinkling stars.

"Okay, Charlie, you're the smart one. You ain't anymore loco than the rest of us. Tell us what you think." A thin ribbon of smoke tinged with the faint scent of coal oil snaked around them. Specks shuddered.

"Well, I think there's a difference between a ghost and a spirit."

"Haints is haints," Specks said. "And they scare the daylights out of me. What's the difference?"

Charlie paused and stared into the darkness. "I think ghosts walk around and haunt places because they're lost or confused."

"There ain't nothing to be confused about. They're dead," Jesse said.

"That's just the point." Charlie slapped his knee. "They may not know they're dead.

Maybe they died so fast, they don't realize it. Some of them may know it, but don't want to let go because they have something left to do, or have loved ones they don't want to leave. For all we know, they could be scared to go on. They're stuck between worlds. They're bound and aren't free to go."

"Damn, Charlie," Jesse said. "I ain't never heard anyone talk about ghosts like this. You act like they're people."

"They were...once." Charlie laughed. "Spirits, on the other hand are full of joy. They're free and live in constant happiness and peace. No fighting. No war. They live surrounded in pure love all the time."

"*That* would be Heaven," Jesse said.

"That corporal died quick. Think he's already a ghost?" Specks looked over his shoulder into the frosty dark and shifted closer to the light. "Wonder if he's in Heaven?"

The smoking lantern lured a small moth to its red-flamed mouth. Specks reached over and shooed the delicate insect away before the heated tongue of the lamp caught and burned its wings. "Seen enough death today," he explained.

Charlie nodded in understanding.

"I don't want to go to Hell, Charlie," Specks said.

"Quit thinking of Heaven and Hell as an actual place. I think it would help if you just thought of them as a state of mind."

"Huh?"

"Hell is torment. Violence. Hate. Heaven is peace, joy, and compassion. Neither are places. They're emotions. You choose which ones you want in your life."

"If I'm followin' your line of reason," Jesse spoke up, "then we make our own Heaven and Hell right here, right now." His brow knitted into a thoughtful frown. Pointing at Charlie with his cigarette, he said. "You've got a good notion there, Charlie. Never thought of it that way."

"Yeah, Charlie," Specks said. "I like your way of thinking a whole lot better than that ol' windbag Reverend Harris. He prided himself on scaring people with his preachin'. I remember one Sunday he got to yellin' and hollerin' about our transgressions and the fury of Hell. I was only ten. Didn't have no idea or even cared what transgressions was. Jenny Thompson sat in front of me. She had her hair done up in pigtails, and I couldn't resist pulling on them. Harris pounded and beat the pulpit with his Bible so hard he broke out in a sweat. That Bible slipped from his wet hand, flew across the pews, and hit me upside the head. I damn near pissed down both legs. For weeks I went around thinking it was a sin to pull a girl's hair, and I was doomed to an eternity of fire and brimstone."

"Oh, Lord, Specks, I'd forgotten about that." Jesse laughed. "I got so damned tickled I wanted to bust out laughing. I knew Ma would whup me good for laughing in church, so I held it in. But when your face turned white as egg shells and your eyes got bigger than tin plates, I thought my guts was gonna bust. That pinned up laugh turned into tiny farts. Sounded like hail on a tin bucket when they hit that wood pew. Emmie laughed so hard, she fell on the floor. Ma's face turned the color of boiled beets. She stomped up the aisle and outta that church faster than a bobcat chasing a rabbit."

Charlie broke into hard laughter. Specks rolled on the ground, holding his sides. Tears streamed down Jesse's face. Gasping for breath, Charlie looked at Specks. "Laughing is Heaven at its best."

"Then dying won't be so bad," Specks said.

Chapter 23

"What's your name, boy?"

Emmie's heart pounded. Three days and three cold nights had passed since she'd run headlong into the moonlight determined to find Jesse, but it seemed longer. She'd been lucky that first night, stumbling onto a group of men heading south to enlist. Staying just out of eyesight, she tagged behind them. Not wanting to be seen, she camped without a fire. Burrowed deep inside the wool blanket, she ate her bread in silence and nursed her sore feet. Jesse's boots were too big and without socks, they'd rubbed blisters on her heels and big toes. During the day, while walking for miles, she rehearsed the story she would tell until she knew it frontwards and backwards. But now that it was time to tell it, her mind went blank.

The burly lieutenant shifted his weight and stared. It was his fault. The wad of tobacco packed in his cheek made his straggly goatee jiggle with each chew. He reminded her of the Widow Thompson's prized billy goat, Rufus. His watery blue-gray eyes and dull look added to the image. She drew in a deep breath. Whew! He stunk as bad as Rufus, too.

"I said, what's your name?"

"Timmy. Timmy Brown."

"Well, Timmy Brown, you don't look any older than a fresh-weaned pup. The Confederacy isn't desperate enough for men to rob the cradle just yet. Go back home to mama."

Panic shot through her. She hadn't counted on this. Anger smothered her fright. Her feet burned. She'd eaten the last of the bread before sun-up, and now the sun was slinking out of sight. Tired. Hungry. And desperate. Damned if she'd let this stinkin', tobacco-chewin' goat man turn her away.

"I ain't got no Ma."

A stream of tobacco juice leaked out of the corners of the lieutenant's mouth and slowly traveled down his chin. He wiped the dribble away with the back of his hand. "Whatcha mean?"

His stupidity broke the ice on her memory. "My ma's dead. Pa runned off. Me and my brother been livin' in an orphanage. When he heard about the war, he runned off, too. Ain't no way I was goin' to stay there without him, so I runned away to find him. I ain't goin' back. If'n you don't let me join up here, I'll go till I find a place that will."

The lieutenant's mouth split into a wide grin. He ran his tongue over his yellow stained teeth and spit. "Ya got guts, I'll say that for ya. What's your brother's name?"

"Jesse Brown."

He looked into the black ledger book and shook his head. "Don't see his name here, but that don't mean nothin'. Lots of places he could go to join up." Glancing up from the book, he studied Emmie. "I ain't gonna send no kid, no matter how young, back to one of them homes. Heard they can be hell. I'll take a chance on ya, but ya gotta pull your own weight. This here is a supply unit, and we ain't got time to raise no baby. Savvy?"

"He can help me."

Emmie turned toward the voice. A short, round man with a stained apron tied around his waist, hiked to the table. "You been promisin' me a helper ever since I joined this outfit. This kid will do fine. Okay by you?"

"Kid, this here's Henry, our camp cook. From now on you work with him. Can ya write?"

Emmie shook her head. "No."

The officer wrote Timmy Brown in the ledger. "Make your mark by your name. Congratulations. You're officially a soldier in the Confederate army."

"Come on, kid," Henry said. "Hungry? I think we got enough beans left to fill ya up. Gotta put some meat on them bones if ya gonna be any help to me."

Emmie limped beside the heavy cook and sighed in relief. Lady Luck was still on her side. Henry's cook wagon sat off from the core of the camp and loomed like a giant hulk in the half-mooned night. A thin finger of smoke from the cook fire pointed to the starlit sky, and the smell of coffee and hot food made her mouth water.

"There's some warm beans in that pot, there," Henry said, and pointed to a large kettle resting on the coals. "Got a couple of biscuits left, but they're cold. Coffee's hot, though. Help yourself."

While Emmie crammed beans and biscuits into her mouth, Henry poured a cup of coffee and sat down beside her. She felt his gaze and turned her face into the shadows. Henry chuckled.

"Now, baby girl, tell me your true name and what you're really up to."

The biscuit turned to hardtack in Emmie's mouth

and she choked. It was a bluff. Had to be. How did Henry know she was a girl?

Stay calm.

"My name's Timmy, and I ain't up to nothin'."

"Uh, huh," Henry said. He stood, hitched up his trousers, and walked to the cook wagon. Under lowered lids Emmie watched him rummage through the pots and pans until he pulled out a bottle.

"When you're done eatin', grab that pan of dishes and take them down to the creek. Might as well start earnin' your keep around here."

She waited until Henry disappeared in the mist, then let out the breath she'd been holding. Her luck had run out. He'd noticed something that made him suspect she was a girl. But what? And what was in that bottle? Whiskey? Sure didn't need him gettin' liquored up and shootin' his mouth off. She better hurry with them dishes.

Wolfing down the rest of the bread, she jumped up and hobbled over to the pan. What was worse, walking all day on sore feet, or sitting a spell, then walking? Either way she limped like a foundered horse.

The bushes grew thick, and the night closed in around her. Frogs croaked in deep voices and a coyote yipped in the distance. Emmie shivered, but not from the cold. The night was too dark. Should've brought a lantern, but she thought Henry would be closer. How far downstream had he gone? The sound of splashing water and a dot of yellow led her to a secluded spot surrounded by trees that stood like tall, leafy guardians with long, wooden arms. Clothes hung from one of the lower branches. Emmie's heart leaped.

Henry was buck naked!

She scurried back into the dark. Maybe he hadn't seen her.

"Come on in, kid. The water's nice and cool."

Damn!

"Huh…no thanks. Think I'll just wash up these plates and head back to camp. I'm kinda tired."

She heard a low chuckle.

Skirting past the clothes, Emmie kept her gaze trained on the creek bank. A honeysuckle-flavored breeze stirred the air and blew a piece of clothing off the tree. The garment sailed to her feet.

Oh God! Oh God! It was his bloomers!

Oh God!

Wait.

Bloomers?

The low chuckle turned into a laugh.

"What's the matter, kid? Ain't never seen a pair of lady's bloomers before?"

"Not on a man."

"There ain't no men here, baby girl," Henry said and stood.

The pan of dishes crashed to the ground.

Henry had tits!

"Throw me that towel, yonder," Henry said, and walked toward the shore

"You're a woman?" Emmie watched Henry wrap the cloth around him…uh, herself.

"Yep. From head to toe."

Emmie sank to the ground and said nothing.

Henry took the bottle from under the tree and walked toward her.

"Take them boots off."

"Huh?"

"Your boots."

In a daze Emmie pulled off the boots and winced. The blisters had broken and weeped slimy water.

"Woo-eee, baby girl. No wonder you walk like you got a cob up your butt. Stick them feet in that creek water. While they soak, we'll have us a talk. Just let me get dressed."

The cool water hit the soles of Emmie's feet like a slap in the face, and she jerked them back.

"Stick 'em back in."

Emmie leaned back on her arms and forced her feet into the water.

Henry, fully-clothed, eased down beside her. "Your ma really dead?"

Emmie sighed and surrendered. No sense in lying. "No. That part of the story weren't true. But Pa did run off, and I do have a brother named Jesse. He run away to join the war." She ducked her head. "My name's Emmie."

"Pleased to meet ya, Emmie. My name's Henrietta Jones."

Emmie shook her outstretched hand and smiled. "How'd you know I was a girl?"

"Takes one to know one." Henrietta laughed. "You ain't got the hands and wrists of a boy. Your fingers are too long and delicate."

Emmie gasped. If Henrietta noticed, then the lieutenant would, too.

As if reading her mind, Henrietta shook her head. "Don't worry, baby girl. These yahoos are too busy scratchin', spittin', and fartin' to pay any attention to you or your hands. Just keep their bellies full and they'll leave ya alone. That's what I do." She cocked her head and stared at Emmie.

"Things so bad at home, ya gotta join the war to get away?"

Emmie didn't answer. In the distance a whippoorwill called for its mate, the most soulful, lonely cry she'd ever heard. "I wasn't wanted. Won't be missed, neither. I joined the army to find my brother. He's the only one what loves me."

"My, my." Henrietta clicked her tongue and patted Emmie's hand. "A mama not wantin' her baby girl. That's a sin if'n ever there was one."

"Who you lookin' for?"

Hazel eyes dimmed to a shade of withered moss and sorrow dulled her glow to dried parchment.

"No one, baby girl. I lost my man and young'uns to the fever. Buried them myself, underneath the sycamores."

Emmie didn't know what to say. The soft breeze turned cool and she shuddered.

"Best get them feet out of that water," Henrietta said, and opened the bottle.

The pungent odor of turpentine and camphor made Emmie sneeze. "What's that?"

"Horse liniment. Gonna dab them sores with it."

Emmie's face paled. "Will it sting?"

"Like you stepped barefoot in the middle of a hornet's nest." Henrietta laughed. "But they'll heal overnight. Just you watch and see. Now, give me that foot."

Tears welled in Emmie's eyes and streaked the dirt on her face when they fell. Her foot was on fire, and she squirmed against Henrietta's firm hold.

"Give me the other one. Hold still!"

Emmie gritted her teeth and asked. "How many young'uns did you have?"

"Two. A boy and girl. Seth and Mattie. Them boots your brother's?"

"Yes, um."

"Thought so. You need socks."

"Don't have none."

"Hmm." Henrietta sighed and laid Emmie's feet in her lap. With a calloused hand, she gently rubbed the soles and toes.

Emmie never felt anything so good.

"Mattie was about your size and age. I'm guessing you be about sixteen?"

Emmie nodded.

"Seth was fourteen. They's good kids. So was Joshua, my man. Never felt so lost and alone in my life after they died. Didn't know what I was gonna do. Then I heard about the army. Paid good money." She elbowed Emmie and winked. "Course, if the South don't win the war, them bluebacks won't be worth a fart in a whirlwind. Don't really care anymore if I live or die, so I went to join up. They refused me. 'Cause I was a woman. Made me madder than a treed bobcat. No one, especially a man, tells Henrietta Jones she can't do somethin'. I marched back home, cut my hair, tied up my titties, put on some baggy clothes, and went back. Changed my name to Henry. Told them I could cook. That's all it took. Now, here I am." She looked at Emmie and smiled. "And here you are."

Emmie grinned back. She'd only known Henrietta for about an hour. But in that time, the woman had shown her more love and attention than Ma had in her whole life.

"Listen to me, baby girl," Henrietta said, her face serious. "It ain't hard foolin' these men. There's a lot more women in this war than they know about. They join up for various reasons. Some want to be with their men. Others want the money. But ya have to be smart. Sleep in your clothes. Take a bath early in the morning or late at night. That won't be hard. Cooks get up before the crack of dawn and work way after sundown. I take the dishes down stream to clean. They think it's so I won't foul the drinkin' water, not because I'm washing up. Don't use the latrines. Pee in the woods. Speak only when spoken to, and answer in short sentences. Understand?"

"Yes, ma'am.

"Can ya cook?"

"Yes'm. Done most of it back home. My biscuits ain't as fluffy as yours."

Henrietta smiled, the light flashed in her eyes, and she winked. "I'll show you my secret to making 'em. Stick close to me. I don't hold much hope in you finding your brother. It's a big army. There's talk flyin' that we're headin' out for a place called Shiloh. But stranger things have happened. We found each other, didn't we? Now, let's get back to camp. Dawn comes mighty early."

Emmie laid underneath the cook wagon and gazed into the dying embers of the campfire. A lazy, smile spread across her face and her eyes grew heavy. Lady Luck was still around, and her name was Henrietta.

Pulling the blankets up to her chin, something soft brushed her hand. Tears filled her eyes.

Two pairs of socks lay next to her pillow.

Chapter 24

"Saddle up, men. You've been looking for a chance to fight. By God, now you got it."

Specks tightened the cinch on Belle and mumbled behind the lieutenant's back. "I ain't been lookin' for no fight. Where we goin' in such an all-fire hurry, anyway?"

"Shiloh," Charlie answered.

"Pretty name. Where's it at?"

"It means peace, and it's somewhere in Tennessee."

"Can't be too bad of a place with a name like that."

"Better hurry. They're forming the column to ride out as we speak."

"Hurry, hurry, hurry. That's all this army knows," Specks said and swung into the saddle.

Tried and cranky, Specks stood in the stirrups. "My butt's sore as a boil."

Gumpy rode up beside him and grinned. "It's only the third day, boy. We got at least nine more ahead of us. But don't fret none. Purdy soon that keester of yours, will just go numb."

Yelling like a wild Indian, Jumper whipped his team past in a whirlwind of dust.

The fine powder settled on Specks' jacket and he swore, "What's his hurry?"

"Oh, Jump likes to have camp set up before we get

there. Always has. It's a matter of pride to him."

Saddle leather groaned in protest as Specks turned and looked at Gumpy. "I've been meanin' to ask. How did Jumper lose his leg?"

Overhearing the question, Jesse and Charlie reined in beside Specks. When Specks saw the look on Gumpy's face, he regretted the question. The peppery sergeant turned as ashen as the trial and laugh lines flattened into a frown. Maybe he shouldn't have asked.

"You don't have to talk about it, if'n you don't want."

His words came slow and drawn-out. "Naawww…I suppose ya have a right to know. Just ain't a purdy story, that's all. Brings back a lot of memories I'd just as soon not poke at."

"Did ya see it happen?" Specks asked.

"Yep."

The dabbled-gray slowed to a walk, and Gumpy waited for them to join him. An eerie hush closed in. The musical jingle of spurs and bridles faded. Even the sharp clip-clop of the horses' hooves dulled to a dull clop, clop. A shiver ran up Specks' spine.

"It were a fight in some far off place." Gumpy's voice turned cold. "Don't recall the name of it, now." The wind stirred and stole the words from his lips. "Strange how time works. I'd bet money I'd never forget. Don't seem to matter that much now."

They rode in silence, then Gumpy cleared his throat and began again.

"Jumper's given name is Wesley. We grew up together. Our mamas called us biscuits and gravy…can't have one without the other."

A low chuckle escaped him. He spit, wiped his

mouth on his jacket sleeve, and gave Specks a hard look, then let his stare rest on each of the other two.

"Confusion runs wild and wooly in battle. One minute things are goin' your way, the next it's the enemy what has the upper hand. That's what happened with us. Jump and me got cut off from our unit. We'd been hidin' and dodgin' Yanks all mornin' tryin' to work our way back to our lines. I was runnin' a few steps ahead when I heard him scream."

Eyes squeezed shut.

"Blood gushed from Jump's leg like a ragin' river after a spring thaw. He fell like he'd been pole-axed. Took my belt and tied off the wound. Threw him over my shoulder and ran."

Specks shivered. He threw Jesse a quick glance.

"Another thing you'll find out in war is how to pray. Me and the Man upstairs became ridin' buddies that day. The good Lord took pity on us, 'cause the next thing I knowed, we found our men. A burnt-out barn was being used as a field hospital."

"Hospital." A snort of disgust. "I use the term loosely. It took half a day for anyone to look at Jump. Heard later that was good. Sometimes it took a whole day or maybe two, afore a doc could help." His voice weakened. "Just too many men."

Specks fought the urge to nudge Belle and pull ahead of Gump. He didn't want to hear anymore, yet he couldn't turn away.

"I gotta hand it to them sawbones. They's few in number but worked non-stop standin' for hours over them operating tables." Again he grunted. "Tables. That's another word I use lightly. They were just rough, splintery boards laid across apple barrels."

He drew the gray up, reached in his pocket, and pulled out a knife. Slicing off a hunk of tobacco, he wadded it in his mouth between the cheek and gum. Chewing hard, he took a ragged breath. "Some men screamed in pain. Some didn't know where they was, kept cryin' for their wives or mamas. Others just laid there like empty husks waitin' for death. They were the worst."

The wind kicked up, and the sharp smell of manure invaded the air as the rest of the column of men and horses filed past. Clouds hid the sun and turned the trees that lined the trail a grim, grayish color. In the distance a crow cried out. The sound of creaking leather sounded two loud when Specks squirmed in the saddle. Damned if he liked the direction this was goin'. It was like Sarge had entered another world, one empty of all feeling.

"This doc in a filthy, blood-stained coat told me Jumper's leg looked like mincemeat pie. A minie ball shattered his lower leg bone. He said he thought he could save some of the leg, but not all. Amputate was what he called it. Butchery was what it was."

Bile erupted in Specks' throat. He forced it down with a gulp and glanced over at Charlie.

Charlie didn't meet his gaze and focused on the spot between Red's ears.

"I heard stories about legs being cut off without nothin' for the pain except whiskey, but Doc said that was more rumor than fact. He promised Jump wouldn't feel or know a thing. The rag he put over Jump's nose and mouth was soaked in somethin' called chloroform.

An ugly grimace crossed Gumpy's face. "That doc took a little bone saw and cut through Jump's leg like he was sawing a limb off a tree. Blood spattered ever'where. Looked like a hog-killin' for sure. Then he took plain cotton thread and sewed up ever'thing nice and neat. Sewed as good as any woman at a quilting bee. Straight. Close. Little stitches. Next, he smoothed off the bone, tied the loose skin over the stump, slapped some jelly-lookin' plaster on it and was done. The whole shebang took less then ten minutes."

With a heavy sigh, Gumpy spit. Brown, thick tobacco seeped into the dirt, turning it into a thin stream of sticky-looking goo.

"Never would've thought a man's life could change forever in that short of a time. Ya know what he did next?"

Tears filled Specks' eyes, and no words came out. Why, oh why, had he asked? He hadn't bargained on all of this. "I ain't sure I want to know."

"He took Jump's leg and threw it on a heap with all the others, like stumps on a woodpile. Legs. Arms. Feet. Hands. Must've been dozens of 'em. Tossed it there and then walked off! Like it was nothin'. A man's leg. The boot was still on, and it laid there twitchin' and floppin' like a fish out of water. Beat anythin' I'd ever see. Made me wonder what kind of men we are to treat each other so." A far-away look captured Gumpy's eyes, and he gazed into the distance, speaking only to the wind.

"I had to leave him there. All alone. First time we'd been apart in years. Damned near didn't go. But orders is orders and I am a soldier, so I went. Jump understood, but that didn't help much. That pile of arms and legs tagged along with me. Haunted my dreams ever' night. Thought I'd go loco." He chuckled. "Then one day, I looked up and there he was, hoppin' toward me like a three-legged jack rabbit. That's when I started calling him Jumper."

"You joshin'?" Specks asked.

"Nope. The doctors told him to go home, but he refused. Said no one would have use for a cripple on a farm. All they'd do was pity him. Said he could accept no leg, but not pity. So he hunted for me. Took awhile. Weren't enough of the old unit left. What was, scattered to the winds. I ended up with the lieutenant and Unit 547. But ol' Jump found me. Yep, by Gawd, he found me. We was biscuits and gravy again."

A low laugh came from Jesse. "The lieutenant didn't want to send him back?"

"Naw. Funny, ain't it? The lieutenant's a strange man. Cold and hard one minute, carin' and understandin' the next. Won't never forget what Jump told him. He said just 'cause there was less of him on the outside, didn't mean there was less of him on the inside. There's more to a man than skin and bones. It's what's in his heart that counts."

"So, what did the lieutenant do?" Specks asked.

"He just stared at him then asked him if he knew how to cook. When Jump said he was tolerable, that's all it took. I've seen one-armed soldiers still in the army, but never any without a leg. Don't know if the lieutenant talked his superiors into lettin' a crippled man stay or if he just didn't ask. Don't matter. All I know is, he handed Jump's dignity back. Gave him a reason to live. That's why me and Jump would follow that man through the deepest, darkest regions of Hell, which I suspect is were we're headed to."

Specks shot Jesse a look. His face paled.

"Ain't been easy for ol' Wesley. His mind plays cruel tricks on him. Says his leg itches somethin' fierce."

Eyes wide Specks blurted, "Even though it ain't there?"

"Yep. Doc gave him some little pills to take when the pain gets too bad, but Jump won't take 'em. Told me he saw too many men get to dependin' on them so much, they went crazy-wild without it. Hell of a note, ain't it? But Jump shore does like his Tennessee sour mash."

With a touch of his spur, Gumpy nudged his horse forward.

An uneasy stillness ushered in early twilight. No branches waved in the wind. Clouds froze in the skies, and birds flew with muted wings. A chill ran up Specks' spine. Amputation sounded worse than death. He lowered his gaze and played with Belle's mane, twisting and untwisting the silky hair in his fingers. "I guess ya never really know a man till ya walk around in his clothes. Jumper's a braver man than me."

Jesse nodded. "I vow, as of this moment, I ain't never gonna talk against Jumper ever again, nor let anyone else, neither."

"That goes for me too," Charlie said.

Still struggling with the thought of having only one of anything, Specks mumbled, "Amen."

Whisperings

It is Christmas. Electric window candles, powered by two AA batteries, sit in every window sill and cast soft, twinkle light into the dark night. I stare at their glow and wonder. The manuscript is six months old. Am I on the right track?

Charlie and the "boys" sacrificed everlasting peace and put all their trust in me to bring their message of love to the world. What if I screw up? What happens if I can't inject their passion and the importance of universal love and acceptance into their words? What if the book is only considered yet another Civil War story? What if it never gets published, or worse, sits on the shelf and is never read? What if Charlie isn't happy with my effort?

Agggh! What-if's are driving me crazy. I walk away from my computer and wallow in self-doubt and worry. The battery powered candle on top of the TV flashes on.

I freeze.

One sure-fire way to tell when ghosts are around is goose bumps. The chills run up my spine, circle my neck, and slide down my arms. They are so intense I fight the urge to throw up. Unexplained tears gather at the corner of my eyes—angel tears.

Charlie and all the men of Unit 547 surround me in the middle of my living room.

My human side doubts and demands proof. "Okay," I say. "If you are really here when I walk back through the room I want the candle to be off."

I continue on into the kitchen, grab a Coke, and turn back toward my office. On the sly, I cast a glance at the TV.

The candle is off.

Still, I balk. "Maybe the batteries are dead," I reason.

My hand shakes when I pick up the candle and unscrew the light bulb.

No batteries at all!

I stand transfixed in the middle of the front room with tears streaming down my cheeks. Not tears of sorrow, but of joy. Charlie reached through the veil and presented me with the greatest Christmas gift of all: reassurance.

I whisper in a voice that trembles with emotion.

"Merry Christmas, Charlie."

No pictures flash in my mind's eye. No emotions hit me square in the chest. Instead, a still, small voice rings crystal clear through the misty dimensions of time.

"Merry Christmas, Ruth."

~R. H. Burkett

Chapter 25

Peach trees?

Charlie didn't understand. Battle couldn't take place in such a serene setting. An expanse of blue blanket covered the sky from horizon to horizon. A gentle breeze nudged sunbeams through the nooks and crannies of the trees not yet full with fruit. The grass waved lazily. Birds of every kind flitted from branch to branch and whistled merry songs. A honking sound drew his gaze upward—a flock of geese winged their way home in their V formation. No, this wasn't right. Violence had no place here. But then, violence was homeless.

What were they about to do? An ambush, the lieutenant called it. The target, a Yankee patrol. A wise, tactical move, or revenge for the attack on Corporal Williams and his men? Surprise was on their side. Victory their reward. A sure thing. In a few moments the peace of this Garden of Eden would be shattered.

Eyes squeezed shut, apprehension flooding his being, he willed his fear to vanish. Sweating hands tightened around the reins and Red threw his head in protest.

Waiting scrambled his nerves and emotions. His heart slammed hard against his chest and beat so loud surely the enemy would hear. Waiting. For what? Hell if he knew. Yet here they were. Like a picket fence of gray, they stood in line and waited.

To his right, Jesse sat like petrified wood in the saddle. Only an occasional biting of his lower lip betrayed his stillness.

Specks stood next. Tense. Chalky white. His blue eyes so round Charlie wondered if they would pop from their sockets.

James checked his Enfield for the tenth time that day.

Charlie caught Tom's gaze and gave him a weak smile.

He tensed.

Red trembled and broke into a fine sweat.

Something was wrong. No wind. No birds.

The peace of the orchard ended with a shriek more terrifying than Charlie could imagine. The sound ripped the air. Hairs on the back of his neck stiffened.

What the hell?

A fireball, spitting flames and belching fire, crashed down line. Cannon balls exploded and shook the earth, deafening the ears. Mesmerized, Charlie watched the scene play out before him. Fruit trees that moments before stood proud and beautiful, shriveled as their leafy arms burned and fell to the earth. The grass burst into an ocean of green flame. Horses, wide-eyed and screaming, reared, their sharp hooves striking out against an invisible foe. They bolted and disappeared into the smoky inferno.

Fire and brimstone had come to the valley.

Black, ominous terror seized Charlie by the throat. An army of blue-coated soldiers swarmed around him like ants. There were so many! Panic swept through him. Red spooked and ran like copper lightning. Charlie gave him his head. Minie balls hummed past his ears like angry hornets.

God! God! Please help! Cover! I need cover. What happened? It was a sure thing. Where was everyone? Christ! They're dead. Have to be. Otherwise they'd be beside me. Sweet Jesus! I'm alone. God! You have to help me!

Two large boulders caught his eye. An entrance large enough for a horse and rider to pass through yawned before him. He reined in and dismounted. Knees buckled, and he grabbed Red's tangled mane for support. Red's chest heaved. Foamy lather covered his withers and flanks. Charlie leaned against him, feeling the heat from the horse's shoulder on his cheek. The smell of fresh sweat and fear filled his nose. Like giant stone guardians, the rocks surrounded them, shielding them from view. Yankee after Yankee ran past, but none glanced their way.

He was safe.

Eyes closed, Charlie stumbled backwards, leaned against the stone, and slid to the ground. Yes, he was safe, for the moment, but a long way from safety. Void of all thought or feelings he sat motionless, blindly staring at his granite shelter. Red nuzzled him, breaking his stupor. With trembling hands, he stroked the horse's forehead and face. Gratitude filled his heart. Had he been afoot, he'd be dead. Red saved his life.

Small pieces of reasoning returned, bringing with them the painful knowledge that he'd run in the face of battle. Excuses jumped like grasshoppers in his mind. *It happened to fast.*

It was chaos. Trees crashing. Cannons booming. Men screaming.

All valid reasons, but they didn't change the bottom line. He ran. A man wouldn't.

He was still a kid.

Still, he could redeem himself. He must find his unit and fight again. Next time he'd be prepared.

The sun was high in the sky when he cautiously emerged from his stony fortress. Death hit him square on the jaw. The valley stretched out like an artist's palette of indigo blue, gun-barrel gray, and blood red. Hundreds of bodies littered the ground like fallen leaves on an autumn day. Not only bodies, but body parts. A hand there. A leg here. Oh, sweet Jesus, a headless torso.

He gagged.

Oh, dear God. The horses. Twisted. Broken. Lifeless. No! Damned if he'd let Red die this way. He pressed his hand to the horse's chest and pushed the promise into the gelding's heart.

The stench of burnt flesh assaulted his nose. Sulfur from the gunpowder attacked his eyes. Blood stained his boots. He wandered, blurry-eyed and aimless. Red followed, head low. The cries of the wounded followed and tormented him. Water! They all cried for water.

Damn! Something tore at his leg! He looked down into the face of a young soldier. "Please. Water," the boy croaked.

Charlie knelt beside him and offered him his canteen. Crimson stained the soldier's coat—a blue coat.

With a jolt Charlie realized he was literally looking into the face of the enemy. But something wasn't right. This face was no hideous, murdering, blue monster. The dying face of a boy whose mother prayed for his return stared up at him. A mother who would wait in vain. Never to call his name or hear his laugh again. Had she stood in the dusty street and watched him ride from her side?

Charlie's eyelids burned, and he fought not to cry.

The boy never drank. He died with his hand still clutching Charlie's pant leg. The tears broke and streamed down Charlie's face, falling on the blue jacket, ironically turning it to gray. Except for the color of their uniforms, there was no difference between them.

All men bleed red.

Charlie jerked free from the death grip, and crumpled to the ground. Mother's words rang in his ears. "No matter how noble the cause, war is never grand."

At that moment, he understood.

This is barbaric.

Stop yelling for water!

Can't breathe.

Have to get out of here.

He swung into the saddle. Where? Where could he go?

Thunder boomed.

Lightning flashed.

Rain poured.

His back hunched over the saddle, he cowered at the fierceness of the storm. The flood came down as if all the angels in heaven wept at once.

There were no more cries for water.

Chapter 26

Drenched and miserable, Charlie let Red wander. Haunted by the young Yankee's death, he fought to keep hold of his sanity. Could've just as easily been him lying dead and forgotten in a pool of bloody muck. Mortality, like a rattlesnake, strikes quickly, without much warning, and bites hard.

Thunder boomed. Or was the racket more cannon fire? Confused and overwrought, he couldn't tell. Red stumbled. Pulling on the reins, Charlie saw it, a large cave hidden by heavy tree branches. He dismounted. Leading Red, he crossed the threshold into an unlikely sanctuary of wet rock and mold. A dank, musty burlap smell greeted him.

Lightning cracked. So did his nerves. He buried his head in Red's neck and broke into tears. He sobbed for the uncertainty of life. For Mother. For the broken horses. And the dead soldiers, North and South. Never had he felt so lost and alone.

Oh, how he wanted to go home.

Something moved.

Adrenaline shot through his veins, halting the flow of tears and self-pity.

There it was again.

He moved toward the sound, pistol cocked and ready.

There. In the corner.

He didn't recognize the lump trying to meld itself with the cave's skin, but he knew the horse standing over it. Belle.

Curled against the rock, knees to his chest, Specks covered his head with his hands and whimpered, "Don't shoot! Please! Don't kill me!"

Relief flowed through Charlie. Thank God it wasn't a Yankee. He holstered his pistol, reached out, and touched Specks' shoulder.

"Lord, God, mister," Specks begged even louder and recoiled against the hard stone. "Don't shoot."

"Specks? It's me, Charlie."

"Charlie?"

He watched recognition seep into hollow eyes and he jumped when Specks lunged at him.

"Charlie! Oh Charlie! Thank God, it's you. I thought you was some crazy Yank comin' in here to kill me."

"You hurt?"

"Naw…"

The death screech of another cannon ball tore through the air and exploded. Specks crawled into a ball and covered his head again. "Oh, God, Charlie. Make it stop. My head's gonna bust wide open." Specks' voice teetered close to the edge of full-out hysteria.

Charlie squatted beside him and placed a hand on his shoulder. "Specks, we're safe."

"Yeah. Safe." His voice cracked, and new tears sprang to his eyes.

"I…I ain't no coward, Charlie. One minute I was watching them geese fly over and the next…oh, Christ. I shot him in the face, Charlie." Specks turned and vomited.

The sour odor caused Charlie's stomach to lurch.

He stood and moved toward Red.

Specks reached out and grabbed him by the leg, triggering flashbacks to the dead Yankee soldier.

"Ya ain't leavin' me, are ya, Charlie? Don't. Don't go."

The panic and desperation in Specks' face sparked Charlie's compassion. "I'm not going, Specks." He put his hand gently on top of Specks' head. "I need my canteen. Both of us could use a drink."

"Yeah, good." Specks slumped against the stone wall. "Water's good. Whiskey be better."

Even though liquor had never touched his lips, Charlie had to agree. He dampened his bandana and handed it to Specks. "Here. Wipe your face. It's a mess."

"Surprised you can see it."

"Candles."

"What?"

"I forgot." Charlie rummaged in his saddle bag. "Mother put a few candles in here." Tears bit his lashes when he loosened the string on the oil cloth. He'd laughed when she put the candles in his bag. God bless her. How did she know he would need them?

The rotten egg smell of a lit match made his nose wrinkle and Belle snort. With careful steps he placed the flickering stubs of wax in the stone pockets of the cave's sides. Soft light cast dim shadows against the walls.

Specks smiled. "Funny how a little light can change things, ain't it?"

A tear slid down Charlie's cheek. That's what Mother had said.

Outside, the storm and battle raged on. Charlie passed the canteen to Specks and wondered what battle he was warring against inside.

Specks ducked his head. "Charlie," his voice fell low. "I kilt a man today."

Chapter 27

The musty, dirt smell of wet rock hung heavy in the air. Specks took a deep breath that shook him to his boots.

"I tried to tell ya before…about shootin' the Yank. He came out of nowhere, chargin' right for me, whoopin' and hollerin' like a wild Comanche. I didn't have no time to think. All that trainin' took holt. Before I knew it, I raised my rifle and shot. Blew the back of his head plumb off." Gagging, Specks covered his mouth with the damp bandana. "I can still see those hollow eyes staring at me."

"You going to be sick again?" A stupid question, but it was all Charlie could think to say.

"Naw. Ain't got nothin' left to come up. I ain't never shot nothin' before. Reckon' some folks would say I was a yellow-belly, but I don't have it in me to kill."

He took a long drink and handed the canteen to Charlie.

"Those captains and colonels don't know what the hell they're a doin'. My book-learnin' is poor, and I ain't had no fancy West Point trainin', but I know two-on-one when it comes runnin' at ya."

"You're not a coward. We didn't belong in that valley. There were just too many to fight."

"It's only a game to those generals. Like checkers.

The battlefield is a big red-and-black board to them. If their men get jumped, they just reach in the box for more. Problem is, someday the box will be empty."

"And all the men…dead."

The soft hiss from a burnt-out candle sent warm paraffin crawling down the cool wall of the cave. It clung to the rock like an icy finger and Charlie's nose wrinkled as the stale, waxy smell of smoke circled his head. His voice came low and hushed. "I never imagined this kind of slaughter. Mother tried to warn me how awful war is. I thought she was making it up to prevent me from going."

A small chuckle came from Specks. "If'in you knowd' how bad it would be, would ya still have joined?"

"No."

"Me neither. I done made up my mind. I ain't stayin'."

A frown scarred Charlie's forehead. What was Specks talking about? Surely, he didn't mean he was deserting? "I'm not sure what you're getting at."

His gaze on the dirt floor, Specks didn't meet Charlie's eyes. "I ain't never goin' to kill another man, ever again. Which means, I can't stay here. I'm takin' Belle and hightailin' out."

"You're talking desertion. They shoot you for that."

Sarcastic laughter ricocheted off the cave's wall. "Well, they'll have to wait in line. The whole damn Union army is ahead of 'em."

Charlie giggled. He couldn't help it. Specks looked up and broke into a fit of laughter.

It ended as fast as it began.

"I'll never be able to get that Yank's face out of my mind. I'll see them vacant eyes ever' night in my dreams. It's one thing to shoot blind into a bunch of 'em, but it's different when you can see their faces. Know what I mean?"

Yeah, he knew exactly. He had his own nightmares.

"Funny thing is, Charlie, the only difference I could see between them and us was their blue uniforms. I bet somewhere, right now, some of them are hidin' out too. They don't want to kill us anymore than we do them. Makes ya wonder what would happen if all of us refused to fight."

"Peace."

"Ya wanta hear somethin' else's that's funny? I prayed today for the first time."

Even in the shadowed light Charlie could see the blush creep up Specks' neck.

"Back home I went to church ever Sunday, but not for the right reasons." A sheepish grin spread from ear to ear. "I went to see the girls. Especially Jenny Thompson."

Charlie laughed and sat crossed-legged in the dirt.

"But today. I prayed. Hard. Know what I learned?"

His gaze rose and captured Charlie's eyes.

"Ya don't have to go to a place with a wood cross on its steeple to find God. Ya don't even have to know fancy words or Bible verses, neither. A prayer is just talkin' to God like he's your best friend. He don't care if you live north, south, east or west, who you are, or how much money ya got. All He wants to hear is what's in your heart. And He listens, any time, anywhere. Even in a dark cave."

Melancholy crept along the cave's floor like a thick fog and weaved through the stone's cracks and crevices. Red stamped his hoof and shifted his weight against Belle. Irritated, the mare reached around and nipped his shoulder. The crack of sharp teeth on skin sent chills racing up Charlie's arms.

Time stood still. Specks broke the spell.

"You gonna tell them I deserted?"

The beginning of a smile tipped the corners of Charlie's mouth. Some men were cut out for war and violence, but Specks wasn't one of them. This was a man who shooed away moths from the certain death of the lantern's flame. It would be a sin to force such a gentle, kind-hearted soul to kill or maim. Damned if he would be responsible for that. Voice soft, he whispered.

"No."

He watched disbelief fill Specks' eyes.

"What are ya goin' to tell them?"

Through bent knees Charlie studied the ground. After a moment he raised his head and looked Specks square in the eye. "I'll tell them I didn't see you on the battlefield."

"That answer's just like you. Honest. But not to a fault. It ain't a lie. Ain't quite the truth, neither, but no matter." He hesitated. "I got one more favor to ask. When the time is right, tell Jesse the truth. Remember when Gumpy told us that he and Jumper were like biscuits and gravy? That's me and Jesse, too. I don't want him thinkin' I'm dead."

"I'll tell him."

"I owe ya, Charlie. Jesse and me should've been brothers. Mama died when I was young. Pa did the best he could, but he didn't really see me. I was pretty much alone until Jesse came along. When his pa lit out, he not only took the horses but any love what was. Jesse's ma shriveled up into a sour, dried apple of a woman. We just took up with one another."

A crooked smile crossed Specks' face. "I'm scared of everythin', but Jesse ain't afraid of nothin'. When I'm with him, I feel brave too."

His heavy sigh echoed through the cave.

"It was my idea to join the war. Jesse made a promise to his sister that he'd always stay and watch over her, but I talked him into coming with me. Told him it would be an adventure." His gaze traveled around the stone cavern. "Some adventure. Hidin' in a hole. Puking."

Charlie laughed.

"I made him break his word, and it gnaws at my gut. He don't say much about it, but I know he feels bad for leavin' Emmie."

"Specks, don't put that burden on yourself. Sometimes it's easier to blame others for what we do. But when it's all said and done, Jesse has to take responsibility for his own actions."

"Yeah, maybe so, but I still feel that I pushed him into this mess. In the back of my mind, I knew men died in war, but I never bargained on this. It don't make sense. I couldn't wait to get out of Calico Rock. Now, I can't wait to run back. Guess it weren't that bad after all."

"Yeah. The grass is always greener."

"Thing is, Charlie, I ain't got nothin' to go home to. I know I can't stay here. But I don't know where to go."

Charlie drew a deep breath. "I do."

Blue eyes loomed large. "Where?"
"My home. Go home. To Mother."

Chapter 28

Water trickling between rocked seams hummed loudly in the stunned silence. With unblinking eyes, Specks gaped.

Ignoring his skeptical look, Charlie rushed on. "You'll like Cougar Hollow. It's a small town, and nobody asks your business. Go to Mother. Tell her I sent you."

"You're joshin'."

"I'm not fooling. You said you owed me. Well, I'm collecting."

"Yeah, but Charlie—"

"Shut up."

His outburst echoed throughout the cavern and back-lashed the rocks, again and again, before sinking into the stone. Red and Belle jerked their heads and snorted. Embarrassed, he lowered his gaze and stood up. Damn. His insides were wound tighter than an eight day clock. He didn't mean to yell, but Specks had to listen.

"You don't understand." Nerves frayed and raw, Charlie paced and raked his hair with trembling hands. "She begged me not to go. Pa died when I was young, and it was just her and me."

"Like biscuits and gravy?"

A half smile struggled to split his lips. "I promised I'd never leave. My heart broke the day I rode away.

She stood there in the street with tears streaming down her face, looking frail and fragile as glass."

The lump in his throat grew large and his choked sob made his voice crack. "I feel so guilty. Don't you see? I deserted her. If you'd just go and watch over her until I get back, it would be such a comfort to me."

"Would she learn me to read?"

His smile broke. "Everything from the Bible to Aladdin's Magic Lamp."

"I always wanted to know how. And write." He chuckled. "Maybe I'd like my name better if'n I could read and write it."

"She'll teach you anything you want to learn. And food. Lord, she can cook a hundred times better than Jumper."

Deep in the cave's belly a rustling of wings stirred and handfuls of bats flew overhead and shot out the door. Specks ducked and swore. "Damn spooky varmints. Hey, hear that?"

Charlie cocked his head. "What? I don't hear anything."

"Yeah, that's what I mean. No thunder. No cannons. Maybe the battle's over."

The last burning candle spit like a cornered cat and cast long shadows across the stone. Red and Belle dozed, head to tail. Charlie yawned. God, he was tired. Every muscle ached. A chill touched his shoulders. He untied the blankets from the back of his saddle and threw one to Specks. Wrapped like a cocoon he slumped to the ground and braced his back against the rock. Eyes heavy, he pushed Specks for an answer before sleep overtook him.

"So, what'ya think?"

"It's tempting."

"If you're worried about Mother asking questions, don't be. If you want to talk, she'll listen, but she'll never ask why you left the army…she'd be the mother you never had."

That remark must've hit home because unexpected tears rolled down Specks' face.

"I'd like that." Voice soft, he dabbed his eyes with the edge of the blanket. "A man'd be a fool to throw away a second chance like that. Okay, I'll do it."

"Now I owe you."

"Naw, we're even. Charlie? Don't you want to come with me?"

Oh, God, yes. To feel Mother's hand on his head, sit at the homemade table, drink morning coffee bathed in golden sunlight. To smell bacon sizzling in the skillet, and know he was loved and safe, would be a dream come true. But Mother deserved a man to watch over her.

"I can't. Got to prove something to myself first."

Specks didn't question him, and Charlie drew a deep breath. Good. It was too much to explain. Exhausted, he closed his eyes and fell into a deep sleep.

Charlie woke with a start. Where was he? How long had he slept?

Stiff and cold, he rubbed sleep from his eyes. Across the floor, burrowed deep in his blanket, Specks turned and snored. Sunlight filtered through the cave. Charlie nudged Specks awake. "Come on, sleepyhead. We're burning daylight."

"Wish I had some of Jumper's coffee."

Specks grumbled and led Belle out into the dawn. Charlie followed with Red and blinked in the morning light. An eerie stillness surrounded them. No wind. No birds chirping. Nothing. Just dead silence. Charlie reached into his pocket. "I need you to do one more thing for me, Specks."

"Hey, ain't that Tom's pocket watch? How'd you end up with it?"

"Won it. Remember when we first got our horses? I bet Tom that Big John wouldn't last two minutes on ol' Crow." He grinned. "It was a safe bet. Tom knew I'd keep the watch and give it back to him when we got home. I want you to give it to his pa, under one condition."

"Well, sure, be happy to. But what's the string attached?"

"Trade the watch for Mother's wedding band."

"What?"

"Mother gave Tom's pa her wedding band to buy Red with. It's the only thing she had left of Pa's, and I swore to myself I'd get it back for her. Don't give the watch to Harvey until you get the ring. Understand?"

"Good lord. That ma of yours must be some woman. Don't worry, I'll get the ring."

Now that it was time to go, an awkward sinking feeling settled around Charlie. He offered Specks his hand. "Thanks, Specks, for everything. Take good care of Mother. Tell her I love her. I'm counting on ya."

Specks shook back and grinned. "I won't let you down, Charlie. I promise. See ya when you get home."

Charlie reined Red into the sunrise. Sadness rode beside him.

He doubted he'd ever see Specks again.

Whisperings

I live in a quiet mobile home park for retirees. Not that I'm retired, darn it all. Every morning I crawl out of bed and face the 8-5 insanity, while my neighbors enjoy days full of blissful freedom. The park sits in the middle of the woods, like someone picked it up and plopped it there. I share the tranquility with deer, rabbits, raccoons, and gentle folk.

Except for three cats, my house sits empty while I'm at work. I never worry about personal safety even if I arrive home after dark. Flashing lights from sheriff's cars at my neighbor's home shake this confidence.

"What happened?" I ask.

Both of my next-door neighbors' houses were broken into and robbed. In broad daylight.

"We were only gone for a few hours," my neighbor laments. "Whoever did this knew our habits and schedules."

They would know mine, too.

My hands tremble when I unlock the front door. A deputy stands by my side, alert and ready. I switch on the lights. Everything is perfect. Nothing out-of-place or missing.

"You're lucky," the deputy says.

The fluke incident leaves me cautious and curious. I install motion detector lights, triple-check my door locks, and am more observant. Still, I wonder why my house wasn't touched.

The answer comes to me in a dream.

Dreams give solutions to everyday problems. The conscious mind never shuts up during the waking hours. Sleep muzzles the constant barrage of thoughts and gives the subconscious mind a chance to talk. The subconscious uses symbols and pictures to speak. The key to interpreting dreams isn't found in any dream interpretation book. The secret is to figure out what the images mean to you, personally. For example, if I dream of a horse, it means freedom and happiness. My brother hates horses. If he dreams of one, it means something quite different. Sometimes, however, dreams are clear-cut and leave little doubt as to their message.

In my dream, thirty-five Confederate soldiers surround my house. They stand at attention with carbines by their side. Two stand guard at both my front and back door.

I have a private army that watches over me. Phantom soldiers who don't need sleep or food and are always on duty. Alert to everything and anything that goes bump in the night and dedicated to keeping me safe.

Peace of mind is priceless. My gratitude is endless.

Ghostly guardians—I never leave home without them.

~R. H. Burkett

Chapter 29

Fear's ice cold fingers squeezed Emmie's heart and hammered her chest with terrified fists. Her mouth opened, but the shout never came. She couldn't breathe. Smoke attacked her eyes. Frantic, she wiped at them with the sleeve of her torn jacket. The noise! Cannon balls ripped the air, and the earth quaked in agony when they hit the ground, throwing dirt and mud like shrapnel into her face. Henrietta's hand on the top of her head pushed hard and forced her to the bottom of the wagon bed.

"Hold on, baby girl!" she shouted. "Keep down!"

The cook wagon bounced and threatened to tip over. Cast iron pots and skillets slammed into its side, wood splintered. The coffee pot flew through the air like a winged weapon, missing her face by inches. She covered her head with her arms and prayed.

Lord, God. They weren't supposed to be here. That morning they'd received orders to move the supply train north, to Shiloh, but Henrietta refused to be hurried. The unit moved out ahead of them. In their haste to catch up, they missed a turn, and the battle closed in around them. If only they'd left with the rest of the unit, she'd be safe behind the lines.

Terrified, Emmie peeked over the wagon's side. Trees burst into flame from a barrage of fireballs, and the heat suffocated her. Fighting for a breath, she turned her head in time to see Henrietta drop the reins and clutch her chest. A red stain broke through her clasped hands and covered the front of her jacket.

NOOOOO.

Horses bolted. The wagon swerved and flipped over. Emmie slammed into the ground.

Blackness surrounded her.

Was she dead? No. Her head wouldn't hurt if she was, and it pounded as hard as the cannon balls that beat the dirt with relentless fury. She rolled to her knees. A body lay a few feet in front of her. A wave of nausea washed over her, and she crumbled to the ground. Tears streamed down her face.

Why? It wasn't fair. Henrietta had taken her under her wing and loved her like a daughter. This stupid, damn war killed her. Damn it! It should've been her instead. Why was she still alive?

Even as the cries shook and dulled her senses, she knew. Jesse. Somewhere, out there, he waited for her. She must find him. But not today. She didn't have the strength.

She curled into a ball and wept until no more tears came and her throat burned like a skinned knee.

Footsteps sounded behind her. Rebel or Yankee?

"Come on, Earl. We gotta search the area and bring back any wounded. All these dead bodies give me the willies. Hurry up."

A leg stepped over her. A blue leg. Eyes squeezed tight.

A low moan sounded.

"Hey, Earl! Over here. I found one alive!"

Through half-opened eyes Emmie watched the soldier kneel over Henrietta's body. Her breath caught.

Could she be alive?

"For Christ sake's, Jack. He's a Johnny Reb. Leave him."

"No. Captain said to bring back anyone that was alive, friend or foe. Help me tear his jacket off and plug the hole in his chest."

Emmie heard the rip of cloth.

"Holy Mother of God. It's a woman."

"Come on, Earl. Help me carry her to the wagon. Ain't gonna leave no woman out here to die."

"Holy, shit. The captain ain't gonna believe this. What ya think they'll do to her? I mean, when she's patched up and well?"

"Cap won't send a woman to no prison camp. More than likely, he'll tell her to go on home and that'll be the end of it."

Should she show herself? If they'd let Henrietta go for being a woman, then they'd let her too, wouldn't they? Of course she'd never take the place of Henrietta's real daughter, but it would almost be the same. They could be a family. It would be a dream come true.

Jesse's face flashed before her.

No. As much as she loved Henrietta, she loved Jesse more. After all, she'd joined this war to find him. She'd come too far to quit now. Fresh tears clouded her eyes. Sure would miss her.

Were there more Yankees? She lay in the dirt and waited, straining her ears for any sound. There was none.

Careful and slow she stood on wobbly legs and gasped at the sight before her. Bodies covered the ground like a blue-gray blanket. Blood turned the dirt to a dull burnt rust. The stench of death engulfed her and its scent carried its message into the air. Buzzards circled above.

She froze. A Yankee on a red roan horse yelled, drew his sword, and charged straight for her.

Run. Her brain screamed at her to move, but her legs refused.

Closer and closer he came. The sun bounced off the saber and blinded her. Even if she could run, there was nowhere to hide.

Damn it. She should've gone with Earl.

Chapter 30

A scream dropped out of the sky.

Charlie's heart leaped into his mouth. Twisting in the saddle he searched for the banshee spirit. No human could utter such a wild, hair-raising sound.

The shriek ripped the air again and a flash of light caught his eye. A Yankee attacked. His sword danced and caught the sunlight like a slender shard of glass. Possessed with a life of its own, the blade hunted for a target. A slim reed of a Rebel soldier stood transfixed in the midst of the field of dead. The sharp edge raced closer.

Damn. Why didn't that kid run?

Charlie's spur found Red's flank. He drew his pistol.

The revolver jerked and numbed his hand.

Bitter gun smoke blurred his vision.

His ears rang.

He reached for the boy.

Arms wrapped tight around his waist.

"Run, Red!"

The horse needed no encouragement. With flaxen mane and tail flying, Red ran like the hounds of hell nipped at his heels.

Had the shot found its mark? Charlie never looked back. He didn't want to know.

He slowed Red and took a hard look around.

Nothing.

"You all right?" He shouted to the boy behind him. "Seen any of our men?"

A thin, shaky finger pointed west. Still silent, the boy held tight. Hot, choppy breaths tickled the back of Charlie's neck. The kid must be too scared to talk. Understandable. His own nerves lacked only a small cut before they split and unraveled.

They rode in silence. Tense and alert, Charlie sat rigid in the saddle. His back muscles cramped and stiffened. Miles passed. The scent of coffee drifted through the air and his heart quickened. Relief flooded through him when he saw gray uniformed men camped around a small campfire. He rode up to the fire.

"Any of you seen 547?"

A long, lanky soldier wiped his dirt smudged face and threw what was left of his coffee into the flames. A thin trail of smoke pointed skyward. "There's a unit down yonder by the creek. Don't know who they are, but they got a one-legged cook with 'em."

"Thanks mister." Charlie nudged Red into a slow lope and headed for the water.

At first glance, his comrades ignored the horse and riders. Then James took a second look and broke into a run, yelling and shouting. "Oh my God. It's Charlie!"

All dropped what they were doing and scurried after him. James pulled Charlie from the saddle and pounded his back. They swarmed him like locusts and fired questions at him faster than he could answer.

"Where you been, Charlie?"

"Thought you were dead."

"How'd you find us?"

"You hurt?"

"We've been worried."

"Who's the kid?"

They turned to gaze at the boy. Blue eyes, wide and round, stared back. He sat silent and solid like a stone statue.

"Don't know. Rescued him from a crazed Yank."

"Come on," Tom said and pulled Charlie by the arm. "Jumper's got coffee. We've just been waitin' for orders."

"Anyone hurt?" Charlie's voice wavered. The "or dead" was left unsaid.

"Naw. Can you believe it? We thought you was. And Specks. We ain't saw hide or hair of him. Jess is worried sick. He stays with the horses most of the time and don't say much."

The boy inched forward in the saddle and picked up the reins. Puzzled, Charlie gave a small laugh. "Well, he and this kid will get along just fine. He doesn't talk much, either."

He looked up at the boy. "Ride down to the picket line. Tell Jess I sent ya. You can't miss him. He's big and…"

Before he finished the sentence, the boy kicked Red into a trot. Charlie shook his head. Something didn't add up with that kid, but he couldn't put his finger on it.

"Tell us where ya been and what happened," James said and pushed a cup of coffee in his hand. He steered him to the fire. "The lieutenant's madder than a ridge runnin' razorback hog. Rumor has it he didn't want us in that valley but was ordered to."

"He weren't the only one," Tom said. "Beauregard didn't want to attack neither, but Johnston made him."

"Yeah, well he paid for that mistake, didn't he? Got shot in the leg and bled to death from what I hear."

The low hum of voices sounded like music to Charlie's ears. He sipped his coffee and glanced from one face to another. How strange war was. Brutal, destructive, and evil, yet it tied men together in a bond more powerful than mere friendship. In their own rough way each loved, worried for, and cared about the other and rejoiced when the lost returned, safe and unharmed. They were more than comrades. They were family. He sighed deep and long, leaned his aching back against the tree that shaded the circle, and closed his eyes.

Safe, at last.

Jesse ignored the sound of the approaching horse. He squatted on his heels and ran his hand down Patch's foreleg. It was warm to the touch. Hopefully it wasn't anything serious, but he'd better make a poultice and apply it to the leg just to be sure. A lame horse was all he needed. He scowled at the dull thud of hoof beats. His horse was hurt. Specks was missing. What next? He didn't want to think his best friend was dead, but tomorrow would make three days since the battle. It didn't look good, and he wasn't in any mood to talk to whoever it was that rode up behind him.

"Jesse?"

No man in the unit called him Jesse. Something about the voice bothered him. He straightened and stared at the boy sitting on Red. Red? What was this kid doing riding Charlie's horse?

"Who's askin'?"

With a shout the boy leaped from the saddle and hurled himself at Jesse, knocking him backwards.

"Jesse! It's me. Emmie."

He pushed back and held the boy at arm's length. No. It couldn't be. The kid was a half foot taller than Emmie, his face too lean and hard. Yet there was something familiar about the way he stood with his hands defiantly on his hips. With a quick intake of breath, he jerked the cap from the youth's head and watched ragged, tawny hair tumble around a heart-shaped face. God Almighty! It *was* Emmie. He pulled her to him and crushed her against his chest. Thin, wiry arms clung to him. The rough, butternut material of his jacket muffled her cries.

Tears streamed down his face and his body shook. His hold tightened. *Ain't never gonna let her go. Not ever again.*

She squirmed out of his grizzly bear arms, gulped, and stepped back. Shameless tears mixed with the mud and dirt on her face and blazed thin footpaths of salty grime across her cheeks.

They stared at one another, not daring to breathe. To believe.

"Thank God, Almighty." He grabbed her flushed face between his hands, gently wiped the grit away with this thumbs, and peered deep into those cornflower blue eyes he thought he'd never see again. "Tell me I ain't dreamin'. How did you get here? Where did you come from?"

Slender fingers wrapped around his and she giggled.

"I'll explain everything, but I gotta sit down first. My legs are shakin' like a new born colt's. Got any water? I'm so dry, I could fart dust."

Chapter 31

Jesse frowned and handed a canteen to Emmie. She was different. Couldn't quite put his finger on it, but she'd changed. Harder, not as trusting. What happened at home that made her leave and what had she gone through to find him?

"Emmie, how'd you get here? Where did you find that horse? He belongs to—

"Charlie. I know. He rescued me."

"Rescued?"

"Don't get your hackles up. I'm okay."

Fear and a touch of anger goaded him. Damn if he liked her easy manner. "What's got into you? You ain't the same."

He watched fire flash in her eyes. She jumped to her feet. He took a step backwards.

"What's wrong with me? Ain't the same? What'd you expect? Been living for three months pretending to be a boy. Had to learn to walk, talk, and eat like one. Thank God it weren't hard, just had to think like a jack ass!"

A grin tugged the corners of his mouth. This was the Emmie he remembered. "Sorry. Tell me what happened."

She flopped to the ground in a huff. "It's a long story."

"I ain't got nothin' but time." He sat across from

her and pushed his worn cap back. "Ain't nobody gonna bother us. They know I'm worried about Specks. He's missin'. Almost three days now. They're staying clear. Go ahead. Tell me."

At first he didn't think she would. He watched her mark circles in the dust with a twig and bite her lip. The pungent odor of horse manure made his nose wrinkle. He shifted down wind. She began slowly and talked to the ground, avoiding his gaze.

"After you snuck away like an egg-suckin' dog…"

His heart slammed against his chest. "Emmie, before you start to boil the tar and gather feathers, I want to say one thing. I've had a lot of time to think about that night. If I could do it over, I would. I should've taken you with me."

"You're damn right you should've!" Her gaze leaped from the dirt and captured his eyes. "Ma went loco and damn near killed me. Threw me out of the house and forbid me to come back. I had nowhere to go, no one to turn to, and no choice but to find you."

Surprised by the tears welling in her eyes and anger in her voice, he gawked at her.

"Walking on bloody feet. Sleeping in the cold. Hungry. Tired. Worried they'd find out I was a girl." She paused for a breath and swiped at the tears sliding down her cheek. "Afraid you was dead." Voice cracking, she fought to hold them back. "I was all alone, never been so scared in all my life. If it hadn't been for Henry, I don't think I'd made it."

"Henry? Who's he? What'd he do?" Dark eyes narrowed. "He touch you?"

He ducked as the empty canteen flew past his head.

"You stupid, dumb, jack ass! Why the worry all of

a sudden? Didn't give a hoot about me when you left me alone to face Ma's fury. What do you care if he touched me? Jealous that I found someone else to take care of me besides you? Henry never harmed a hair on my head. And just so you know, Henry is short for Henrietta." She laughed at his bewildered look. "Yeah, that's right. A woman. There's more of us in this war than you can count."

A picture of Big John in a dress flashed through his mind and he shuddered.

"She was the cook for the supply train I joined up with. Guessed I was a girl right off. She took me under her wing, protected me, taught me how to make the fluffiest biscuits you ever ate..." Her voice broke. She buried her head in her arms and refused to look up.

"Emmie? I'm sorry." He stared at her not sure what to do. "What happened to her?"

"She got shot." A deep sigh shook her body. "Yanks scoutin' for wounded found her. She's probably in some hospital wondering if I'm dead."

"Well, that's good, ain't it?" The look she shot him could've killed. "I mean, it's good that she's alive."

"Yeah. Just wished there was a way to let her know I'm all right and that I found you. She cared for me like I was her own kin." Glancing at him, she shook her head. "It's strange. Never would've thought I'd find someone that loved me that way in the middle of this hateful war. She always said things happen for a reason. Maybe you leavin' the way you did had to be. It forced me to go too. I found her and for a short time I knew what love was."

A sorrowful smile pulled at her lips. "All my life I blamed myself for Ma's hatefulness. Figured I'd done some awful thing and that I deserved it, but Henrietta made me see that it wasn't my fault. She made me feel good about myself."

Blue eyes pierced the space between them. "It's awful not being loved by someone else and thinking you're no better then dirt. I swear my young'uns will never know that feeling. I'll throw buckets of love over them till they're dripping wet with it. Just like Henrietta did to me."

He tilted his head and studied her, hard. These words didn't come from a young girl, but from a grown up woman. That was it. That was the difference. She wasn't a kid anymore. And yes, he was jealous, but not for the reason she thought. True, he'd felt a twinge of bitterness thinking another man had taken his place, but in the back of his mind he always knew he couldn't protect her forever. No, he was envious of the love a stranger had given her. Would he ever know anything like that?

The wind tugged her hair and flipped it into her face. He laughed. "Who cut your hair?"

"Me." Her smile broke and once again, she was his little sister. "Didn't have no mirror or proper scissors." She spit on her hand and slicked the choppy locks back in place. "It don't look that bad."

"Not if you're a wild and wooly mountain man."

"Jack ass."

Sadness curled around his heart and ruined the fun of the teasing. How he wished she was home. She didn't belong in the middle of the killing and blood.

"Emmie, I understand why you left, but you shouldn't have come here. This war, is…well, it's worse then anything I could've ever made up. It forces you to do bad things. Turns you mean. Makes you kill. I can't protect you from it. It's bigger then me…or you."

Long legs uncrossed, he stood and walked over to the picket line. Gently reaching out he stroked Patch's nose and struggled with his feelings and words. The wind carried the scent of coffee. His stomach growled. "Even so, I won't deny I'm glad you're here. Been worried sick about you. It's just—

"Shut up!"

With cat like speed she leaped from the ground, fists clenched at her sides. "Been through hell finding you. I ain't gonna lose you again. We're blood. Blood sticks together no matter how bad things get. Another thing Henrietta always said was 'two heads are better then one.' We can watch out for one another." She gulped for air but stood her ground.

"I ain't leavin' no matter what you say. Now, go tell them I'm your kid brother. It'll work, Jesse. Been doing it for months. I just keep low and don't talk much."

Wide shoulders sagged. He surrendered. "Ok, you win. Stragglers join us all the time. Course everyone will think hell froze over when I tell them we found one another. But no one will care. Except maybe the lieutenant. Even since the battle he's been acting goosey. Come on. Let's get this over with."

Arm around her shoulder he headed toward camp.

All thoughts of Specks faded into the dark.

Chapter 32

Specks twisted the rim of his cap and stared at the woman standing in front of him. Clara Ely was smaller than he'd pictured, but just as tough. Better be straight with her. Even though kindness filled her eyes, they were hawk sharp.

The ride to Cougar Hollow took longer than he'd counted on. Yankee patrols were thick as fleas on a blue-tick hound. To stay out of sight, he'd ridden miles out of the way. He didn't mind. It gave him time to think about what he'd say to Charlie's mama. The words stuck in his gullet. He hadn't bargained on those stabbing, hazel eyes.

"You have news about Charlie? Is he hurt?"

"Oh, no, ma'am, nothing like that." He watched relief smooth worry lines from her face. "Charlie's just fine. Or, at least he was the last time I saw him."

"You look like you've ridden a long way, Mr…?

"Specks."

"Well, Mr. Specks, please come in. I was about to have some tea. Won't you join me? Please, tell me everything about Charlie." She fixed him with a dead on stare. "How do you know him?"

Damn those eyes. Didn't miss nothing. They pierced his skin and looked into his soul. Made him gawky and uneasy.

Pulling at his frayed collar, he trailed after her like

a floppy-eared pup, his steps big and clumsy. Whew. He'd spent days on the trail and he smelled of sweat, dirt, and horse. He slicked back his hair as best he could and ducked through the door. The scent of fresh-baked bread made his belly grumble, and he saw her brows arch at the sound. Heat raced up his neck, and he coughed to cover up the grumbling. Couldn't help it. It'd been days since he'd eaten anything other than hardtack.

"I rode with Charlie, for a while."

His hand shook and tea sloshed into the saucer when he took the small cup from her.

"Oh, dear, don't worry about that. It's been a long time since I've served tea to a man. I've forgotten how large their hands are. Let me get you a proper sized mug. Would you like some bread and butter? Just came out of the oven. Hot and fresh."

"That'd be mighty kind of you, ma'am, but don't go to no trouble on my part."

The crooked smile on her face told him she knew he was lying. Trying to be polite. Truth was he wanted to cram the whole loaf in his mouth.

Two cups of tea and five slices of bread later, he wiped the back of his hand across his lips and sighed. "Mrs. Ely, that was some mighty fine grub. Best I've tasted in a coon's age. Charlie said you could cook."

"Please, Mr. Specks, call me Clara."

"Sorry, can't do that. Mama always told me to call my elders mister or missus. But it'd make me feel a whole lot better if you just called me Specks."

"All right. Specks it is. Now, please tell me everything about Charlie. It's been months since that awful day he rode away. I've been worried sick. Are you sure he isn't hurt?"

The fear in her face softened his voice. *Must be nice to have a mama to fret over ya.* "He's fine as frog's hair."

"You said you rode with him?"

His heart fluttered. Sure didn't want her to know he'd run away from the Army. Had to be careful what he said.

"I didn't know him long but sure did like him. Told him I was riding this way, and he asked me to look you up. I got messages for James's and Tom's folks, too."

"Oh, Alice will be thrilled! Ol' Harvey Carpenter will be too, but you'll never know it."

"Ma'am." Specks grinned. "Tom said his pa didn't talk much."

Without warning she reached across the table and grabbed his hand. He jumped.

"Specks? How is Charlie, really? I don't mean physically. He was…troubled when he left here. Searching. Lost. I've tossed and turned many nights wondering if he'd found what he was looking for."

Lord. Her pain stabbed to the quick. "I'm sorry, Mrs. Ely, I don't know nothing about that. Once he told me he had to prove something to himself. Never said what that was. But Charlie's the smartest fella I've ever knowed. He'll figure out what ever it is that's bothering him." Rough, dirty fingers curled around her hand. "He told me the day he rode away from here was the worst of his life."

Tears filled her eyes and dulled their sharpness. She pushed back from the table.

"Would you like more tea?" Her voice wavered.

Another cup of tea was the last thing he wanted,

but it filled the silence between them. He watched her, thinking hard. Clara was a proud woman. Wouldn't be the kind to accept help if she thought it was pity. Somehow he'd have to come up with a way to make his staying sound like her idea.

"Alice and Albert are visiting her sister this afternoon and won't be back till evening. I know she'd want you to stay awhile, rest up, and tell us more about Charlie and James."

Specks dipped his head. "I'd like that, but I ain't got no money for a room."

"Nonsense. Who said anything about money? Why don't you take your horse down to the livery and meet Harvey while I get a room ready for you."

Specks fingered the watch in his pocket. "I do need to talk with Mr. Carpenter about...Tom."

"Good, it's settled then." She filled the teakettle. "By the time you get back this water should be hot enough to wash up with." She eyed him from head to toe. "You aren't as broad across the shoulders as James, but just as tall. I'd wager I can find some fresh clothes of his for you to wear till we can get yours washed. I know Alice won't mind. Now, get on with ya, I got things to do."

Specks smiled. Hadn't been with her but a few hours and she was fussing over him like a mother hen. Felt good.

From behind the dining room curtains, Clara watched Specks untie his horse and climb into the saddle. What a sweet, young man. Rough around the edges and shy, but well mannered. From the moment her hand had touched his, she'd felt his compassion. But there was emptiness in his heart. Like Charlie, he was lost and searching, trying to find out who he was. Maybe Charlie had sensed this and had sent Specks to her hoping she could help him. But Specks had pride, so she'd have to convince him it was his idea not to leave.

A small smile crossed her face and she hummed to herself while she climbed the steps to the rooms upstairs. How nice to be needed again. She'd think of a way to get Specks to stay.

Chapter 33

Washed and wearing clean clothes, Specks eyed the dinner table like a cat stares at a rabbit hole. The smell of crispy chicken, fried potatoes, greens, and hot biscuits dripping with butter made his head spin. The urge to reach out and grab a golden-skinned chicken leg burned down his wrist to his fingers, but he held back. Wouldn't be polite. He sat on his hands and waited for Albert to finish saying a long winded grace.

Clara, Alice, and Harvey Carpenter, who had reluctantly accepted the invitation to dinner, sat with bowed heads and folded hands. Hearing news about her son, Alice had burst into tears and hugged him so hard he thought his ribs would bust. Harvey had said little but hung onto every word he told him about Tom. He patted his pocket making sure Clara's wedding band was safe. Harvey had exchanged the ring for his pocket watch with a tear in his eye and a bent smile. Said Charlie needn't have worried. He always intended to give the band back to Clara when the time was right.

Did Charlie, Tom, and James know how lucky they were? To have folks that worried, loved, and prayed every day for their safe return? A tiny smile split his lips. If they didn't, he'd make sure they did the next time he saw 'em.

Good family shouldn't be taken for granted.

"Specks, help yourself. Don't be shy. There's

plenty more where this came from. I got so excited over news of James, that I got carried away and cooked too much. Clara even made an apple pie."

Pie? God almighty. He'd done died and gone to heaven.

Harvey wasted little time in leaving after the meal. The ol' horse trader had been more uneasy at supper than he was. Fearing he would be asked why he wasn't in the Army made him jumpy. Thankfully the topic hadn't come up. However, talk about Clara's farm had, which gave him an idea.

"Charlie told me you had a nice place."

"I suppose to some folks it isn't much, but it's home to me." Clara's eyes misted over. "Been awhile since I've seen it. Harvey rides out and checks on it ever so often, but never when I can go with him."

This was the opening he needed.

"I'd sure like to see it and would be glad to take ya, ifn' you wanted to go."

She fussed with the linen napkin in her lap and didn't answer right away. Maybe he'd overplayed his hand.

"That's kind of you, Specks. I'd enjoy that very much."

He climbed the steps to his room, pleased with the way step one of his plan had worked out. Burrowed deep into soft, clean blankets, he sighed. How long had it been since he'd slept in a bed with sheets that smelled like fresh, summer rain? His face clean? His belly full? Eyes heavy, he fought sleep until he thanked God for sending him to Cougar Hollow and Clara.

In her room down the hall, Clara unbraided her charcoal hair and brushed the gray ringlets with a shaky hand. Not sure how she would feel seeing her home again after so many months almost made her refuse Specks' offer. Staying with Alice and Albert had been a blessing. Helping with the boarding house chores and teaching school took her mind off Charlie and the way it had been. But at night, with silence her only company, she allowed herself to remember the quiet evenings in their cozy cabin. She missed Charlie's laugh. His voice. The safe feeling knowing she wasn't alone. Even though she'd prayed every night for a way to return to her home, she had little hope that it would happen. Specks changed all of that. It was a stroke of good luck that he wanted to see the farm. Perhaps, when he saw the cabin, barn and fields, he'd want to stay and work the place.

He well could be the answer to her prayer.

The early morning sun promised a warm day and Specks helped Clara into the buggy seat hoping the rest of his plan would fall into place as easily as the first part.

"I've packed a lunch for us to take," Clara said, and settled the basket next to her. "Ham sandwiches and the rest of last night's apple pie."

He climbed into the seat next to her and grinned. "Mrs. Ely, you keep feeding me vittles like that and I'll be fat as an ol' boar hog before you know it."

"You could use some meat on those sticks you call ribs." She laughed. "I'd forgotten how nice it is to cook for someone who appreciates it."

Cloudless blue skies stretched from horizon to horizon and a soft breeze carried the fishy water scent of Butcher Knife creek that bubbled along side of them. She shook her heard. "The last time I passed this way was quite different. Charlie and I didn't say two words to each other."

"Why's that?"

"He'd just told me he was leaving for war. We got into a terrible argument over it." Lips pressed into a thin line. "We both said things that we'd held onto for quite some time. They needed to be said, but that didn't ease the sting of hearing them." She glanced his way. "I don't think I've heard you say anything about your family, Specks. Where do they live?"

"I come from Kentucky. Ain't got no folks." He clicked his tongue and slapped the reins across the mare's rump. "Mama passed when I was young. Pa's will to live went with her."

"Oh, Specks, I'm so sorry. It musta been hard growing up without anyone to care. However did you manage?"

He tensed. Had to be careful. Telling her about Jesse could lead to other things he wasn't ready for her to know.

"Oh, I managed."

"Kentucky, you say? How in the world did you meet Charlie?"

Sweat rolled down his neck. Sure didn't like the direction this was headed. Ignoring the question, he changed the subject.

"Charlie said you was a school teacher."

"Yes, I am."

"Guess that's why Charlie's so smart. I ain't had any book learnin'. Always been a dream of mine to know how to read and write." He chuckled. "Told Charlie once that maybe I'd like my given name better if I could write it."

"I suspected that Specks must be a nickname. For your freckles, right?" She smiled at his nod. "Would you tell me your real name?"

"Elmer. Elmer Lewis."

"That's good and strong. I like it. Oh, my." Her breath caught. "We're here."

He stopped the mare in front of the squared-log cabin and helped her down. His gaze followed hers across the yard dotted with wild flowers and into the fields that stretched behind the sun bleached barn like a blanket of brown edged in green.

"Oh, dear, look at those weeds, and the fence needs mending, too."

She walked to the door and went in, but he stayed behind. Eyes closed, he drew in a deep breath of rich, moist soil, ripe enough to grow not only crops, but dreams as well.

Nudging the door open, he walked into the kitchen. The sound of her sobs stopped him in his tracks. She sat at the wood table, tears streaming down her cheeks. The sight of her sorrow twisted his heart into a knot. Not sure what to do, he crossed to her side, knelt by the chair, and fumbled for her hand.

"Mrs. Ely?"

The name bounced off the bare walls, sounding cold and stiff. He searched for a softer one.

"Mrs. Clara? Please, don't cry."

"Oh, Specks, you don't understand." Her voice came so low he strained to hear. "Seein' this farm again brings back so many memories. Charlie's father and I poured our hearts into this place. We had such plans. Raise crops...and children...grow old together. But it wasn't to be. Daniel died. Then Charlie left."

Face turned away, she pulled her hand from his grasp and traced the scarred tabletop with shaky fingers. "Charlie grew weary of reading about the world. Wanted to experience it instead. He stayed here only out of loyalty to me. This place was always my destiny, but never his." A weak smile made her voice tremble. "Wasn't right to force him to live my dream, but he was the glue that held it…and me, together. When he rode away into the mist, my every wish vanished with him."

She turned her tear-stained face to meet his. "For the first time in my life, I'm alone and afraid. Who do I hold onto now?"

"Me." He smiled at the puzzled look on her face.

"Mrs. Clara, you said I didn't understand but that ain't true." He stood and walked over to the window, speaking more to himself than to her.

"All of my life, ol' lonesome has stuck to my side like a prickly pear shadow. I fight it off during the day. There's always something to do and people to talk to. But at night, that all alone feeling creeps into my bed and lays cold by my side. Reckon' lonesome don't care about age, 'cause it scares me too."

Not even Jesse knew that secret.

Clara cleared her throat. "That took a lot of courage to admit." Her voice fell soft.

"Ain't never told anyone that. Don't know why you're so easy to talk to and tell what's in my heart. Don't care, neither. Feels good to get it out. For not being kin, you and me are a lot alike. We both got something the other needs. This place is your dream, and having a home like this is one of mine. Why can't we work together to make our wishes come true?"

"You mean, become business partners?"

"Gosh yes, Mrs. Clara!" Words raced and freckles danced. "That's a right fine idea. My fingers itch to dig in the dirt and grow things. I can help out around here, and you can move back home. It's perfect."

"You can stay in Charlie's room until he comes back." The excitement in her voice faded. "Only thing is, I can't pay you for your work."

He laughed. "Money don't buy a purpose to get up in the morning. Belonging somewhere does. Besides, you'd be giving me a roof over my head, food to eat, and someone to talk to after the sun goes down."

"Even still, farming is hard work. A partnership needs to be balanced. To my mind, room and board aren't enough. I'm not holding up my side of the bargain."

"What if ya learned me to read and write? Would that square us?"

"That's an excellent idea." She stood and extended her hand. "We have a deal...partner."

He shook with her and grinned. What just happened? His plan had worked better than he'd ever dreamed.

Sunlight streamed through the kitchen window and flooded the cabin in a warm glow. He picked up the lunch basket and reached inside. "I know we got a lot of work ahead of us. But can we eat first?"

Clara laughed and eased into the kitchen chair. How wonderful to again be sitting at the treasured, wooden table that had seen so many stories unfold over it. God truly did work in mysterious ways. Not only did He provide her with a way to return home, but had given her another son, as well.

She sighed and brushed a tear from her eye.
Her plan had been good.
God's was even better.

Whisperings

Chill bumps are one way to tell when ghosts are present. The reactions of animals are another. Animals, especially cats, are very sensitive to changes in energy.

My cat, Pan is not only my pet, muse, and writing buddy, but my ghostbusting alarm as well. When she darts from room to room, cries as if she's actually speaking English, and watches invisible flies on the wall, it's a sure bet I have company. Charlie and/or Jesse has popped in for a visit.

I've been working on the book for months. I need a break, so I invite several of my friends over for a small party. Pan is a social butterfly. When I have guests, she strolls into the living room as if to say, "Look at me. I'm beautiful with my emerald eyes and silky black coat."

Toward the end of the evening, my friends want to know how the book is progressing.

"It's very comforting to have a group of Confederate soldiers around to protect me," I say.

This sparks a lively conversation about guardian angels. We laugh and start calling Charlie and Jesse, "Rebel Angels."

From out of nowhere, Pan tears through the room.

"They're here," I say and grin.

"Oops, maybe they don't like being called Rebel Angles," a friend says.

Pan walks out from my office with something in her mouth and drops it in the middle of the living room floor. I gasp.

A few weeks before the party, I'd bought office supplies. While waiting in the checkout line, I noticed novelty pencils that have angels with blue colored wings on the tip instead of an eraser. On a whim I bought one. I put the supplies in my office, then promptly forgot about the bag.

Pan remembers.

On the floor is the angel pencil.

The silence is deafening.

"Wow," I whisper, "I think Charlie and Jesse just told us they like their new nickname."

Pan blinks her mysterious, green eyes at us and trots away like it's no big deal she's delivered a supernatural message.

Even in the paranormal world, cats rule.

~R. H. Burkett

Chapter 34

No one moved. The only sound came from the campfire that hissed and spit. Even the birds stopped chirping.

Charlie shook his head in disbelief. He had rescued Jess' brother? What were the chances? A million to one?

Gumpy broke the silence. "Yee Haw! Break-out the corn mash. We got us a cel-ee-bration."

Cheers destroyed the quiet, and the rattle of tin cups echoed through the late afternoon. Jumper hobbled over to the cook wagon and pulled an old brown jug from beneath the seat. A loud pop punched the air and he passed the uncorked container down the line.

"A toast." Gumpy yelled and held his mug high. "Here's to Charlie, rescues, and brotherly love."

Jumper waited his turn, then slung the jug over shoulder and took a long, hard swig. Charlie tipped the cup to his lips and took a swallow. The pecan-colored liquid tore down his throat, burned its way into his stomach, and kicked his guts. Doubled over, he gasped for breath, coughing and spitting, certain he'd never be able to speak again.

Gumpy pounded him on the back. "Puts hair on your chest for sure, don't it boy. Drink up."

"What's this ruckus about?"

All fell silent, except for Charlie. Red-faced and

wheezing, he tried to gather his wits. The lieutenant fixed a long, cold stare on him.

Gumpy pushed a mug of whiskey into his hand. "Well, sir, we're havin' us a cel-ee-gration. Not only did ol' Charlie show up today, but he rescued this kid form a Yankee." He pulled the boy in front of him. "Turns out this young'un is Jess' little brother."

"That so?"

Charlie wiped his mouth on the back of his hand and straightened. The kid was too young surely the lieutenant would send him home. Judging from the scowl on Jess' face, the lieutenant would be in for one hell of fight if that happened.

The officer studied the lanky kid from head to toe. Wide-eyed he stared back, unflinching, a look of determination and down-right defiance in his eye.

In one gulp the lieutenant drained his cup and extended it for a refill. "Strange things happen in war." He walked back to his tent and disappeared into the mist as silently as he'd appeared.

Another fit of coughing seized Charlie. Jess laughed. "Reckon' now that all the excitement is over, me and Timmie will head back down to the horses."

Charlie knew this would be a perfect time to tell Jess about Specks. He followed them to the picket line.

"Looks like I owe you another thank you," Jess said after hearing the news.

"I didn't do anything," Charlie protested. "Specks had his mind made up. I just offered him an unforeseen option."

"Just the same, thanks. Makes me wonder, though. Awful temptin' to send a friend home and not go with him. Why didn't you go too?"

Charlie shifted his weight from one foot to the other. How long would this feeling of being a kid plague him? Even wrestling with the question proved he wasn't grown. A man would just say straight out what bothered him.

"I got something I need to prove to myself before going home. No use talking about it. I just need to stay here for the time being."

Jess nodded. "Well, look at it this way, if'n you'd gone with Specks, you never would've saved Emmie's life."

The name fell heavy between them.

"Emmie? Who's Emmie?"

A small laugh. "You heard wrong. Said Timmie. That corn whiskey got you all turned around. You're hearin' things, now."

That was true. He did feel dizzy and kinda fuzzy. "Yeah, that must be it. Think I'll unsaddle Red, give him a well deserved rub down, then hit the hay."

Twilight stars poked their heads out from the clouds, crickets and bullfrogs began to tune-up for their nightly hootenanny. Where had the time gone? Been quite a day.

"Hey, kid? You left your Johnny bed tied to my saddle. Might have need of it."

He tossed the bundle. String broke. The bag's contents flew to the ground and rolled. Clothes. Blankets. A tortoise-shell mirror. A brush. Bending down, Charlie picked up the mirror and brush. He looked questionably at the items. "Strange things for a boy to have."

"They belonged to our ma." Jess jerked the brush from Charlie's hand. "They be the only things we got of hers. We—

"You're a liar."

The accusation hit hard, like steel against iron. Eyes narrow, Jess laughed, short and dangerous. "Careful, Charlie."

"Specks told me you hated your ma. Doubt you'd keep anything of hers. Besides, I always thought something didn't fit with your brother. Just figured it out. Hasn't got the hands of a boy. Wrists are too delicate and pretty. It wasn't the whiskey. I did hear right. You did say Emmie." He pointed his finger at Jess' brother.

"You're a girl!"

Time stood still. Horses sensed the tension, pawed the ground, and shook their heads.

"Charlie. You can't tell," Jess pleaded. "You don't understand."

"I have to. War is no place for a girl."

Shades of rage washed over Jess' face. Black, cold eyes threw daggers at him.

"Damn it, Charlie! For once, climb down off that high horse of yours."

"What the hell is that supposed to mean?"

"It means that holier-than-thou air you wear like a coat gets awful trying. Not everything is black and white. Right or wrong." He snorted. "Hell, war ain't a place for no body. Man, woman, girl, or boy. Yet here we are. What's the harm if she stays? She's been a part of this thing long as we have."

Jess' words seared through Charlie like a red-hot poker to coals. He paced back and forth trying to control his temper. "It isn't right. What if she gets shot? Or worse. Captured. What if she loses a leg, like

Jumper?"

"Ah, Charlie you know well as me, those things could happen to any of us."

"But we're not women."

Silent up to this point, Emmie snapped. "So what? You think that means you can handle those kinds of things better? Women are tougher than boot leather. Have to be. Who do you think cleans up the messes you high-and-mighty men make? Just 'cause you got an extra part danglin' between your legs, don't mean you're braver or better." She stood next to her brother. "Jesse's all I got. I ain't leaving him."

Dumbfounded, Charlie stared. No one talked like that. If the situation wasn't so tense, he would've laughed. What a little wildcat! A spark of admiration flared, and he gave Emmie a closer look. Kinda pretty, all riled up and red-faced. Anger made the tiny freckles across her nose dance in its heat, and her blue eyes turn a deep indigo. Cut from the same cloth as Mother. Strong. Independent. Tough enough to handle anything. Back home, he'd give serious thought to courting her, but damn it. This was war. Women had no business fighting. It was wrong that she was here.

"I won't do this. I'll keep quiet about Specks, but I won't keep this secret." He turned toward camp heading for the lieutenant's tent. Jess grabbed him and spun him around.

"Can't let you do that, Charlie."

Struggling free from the steel grip, Charlie's temper broke. "Try and stop me."

An iron fist slammed his jaw and knocked him backwards. Tripping and falling over saddles and blankets, Charlie hit the ground hard. Lights, like hundreds of tiny twinkling fireflies, flew in front of his eyes. Blood trickling into his mouth acted like a detonator and ignited his rage. He lunged at Jess' knees.

Jess crashed to the ground landing on his back. The wind left his lungs. Quick as a snake, Charlie jumped on his chest. Squalling like a tom cat he pummeled at Jess. Dust flew. Horses snorted, threw their heads, and whinnied.

On his way back from the privy, James heard the commotion. "Fight!" he yelled. Like bees to honey, men appeared from out of nowhere and surrounded them. Shouting and cheering, they added fuel to the fire.

The lieutenant charged the circle like a raging bull. He hauled Charlie up by the collar and shook him. His voice boomed and the earth quaked.

"What the hell is this? Didn't get enough on the battlefield?"

Jess struggled to his feet.

The lieutenant dropped Charlie and wheeled on him. "I won't have this. Not in my camp. Hasn't there been enough killing going on without you two squaring off like a couple of mad dogs? I'm sick of it! The fighting. The killing. Brother against brother. Fathers against sons. Hate thicker than molasses. The whole damn mess. Don't care who started it. Don't care what it was about. It stops, now!" He looked at Charlie, then at Jess. "Understand?"

Not waiting for a reply, he stomped back to camp. Each step jarred another cuss word from his mouth.

Charlie stiffened and stamped off toward the creek to pout. Insides boiled. God. The itch to hit something, anything burned down his arm to his fist. He flopped to the ground. Damn, his jaw and head ached. Jess' words rang in his ears. Where they true? Was he that self-righteous?

A shadow fell across the grass. Fists clenched.

"Come back for more?"

Expecting to see Jess towering over him, Charlie eyes widened in surprise.

Emmie stood before him. "Here." She handed him a cup. "Thought you could use this."

Suspicious and leery, he took the tin cup from her hand. The scent of bittersweet whiskey wrinkled his nose.

"Didn't bring it to smell. Drink it. Make ya feel better. Settle your innards."

He took a sip, careful of his split lip. How'd she know what his insides felt like? The liquid hit the back of his throat as sharp as a bumble-bee sting, but warmth soon followed. A relaxed, easy feeling flooded him.

She sat crossed legged in the grass opposite him. He stared in disbelief when she pulled makings for a cigarette from her pocket. Long, slender fingers tapped the tobacco in place. Fascinated, he followed her tongue as it slid smoothly across the paper, sealing it tight. She pulled the pouch shut with her teeth and grinned mischievously. "You don't approve?"

"Surprised more than anything. I've never seen a girl smoke before."

Smiling ever-so-slightly, she lit the tip. Tiny orange and red sparks snapped and floated into the early night air. The faint scent of sulfur chased after them. "Ain't a girl. Remember?"

He rubbed his throbbing jaw. "I remember." So this was how it was going to be. The fight was still on.

Only this time words were the weapon of choice. "Did Jess send you?"

Lazy smoke swirled around her heart-shaped face and faded. A warm breeze played with her tousled hair. "No. He knows I'm here, but he didn't send me. Told him I was gonna clean up this mess. After all, that's what we women do."

He tired to ignore her impish grin. Damn, she was arrogant. But pretty, in an obnoxious tomboyish sort of way.

He drank.

She smoked.

Bull frogs burped.

Time waited.

"He's scared of you."

Charlie's brows arched. The tin cup rattled against his teeth. Whiskey slopped over, spread across his hands, and splashed the dirt. "Me? Jess is afraid of me?" He threw back his head and roared with laughter.

"Not your strength, jack ass! We both know he could snap you like a twig."

Her sharp tone stifled his humor. Knowing she spoke true didn't lessen the injury of her slur. He scowled. "Then what?"

"Your book learnin'. Of how smart you are." She pulled on the cigarette. "We ain't had no schoolin'. Neither one of us can read or write worth a lick. Don't bother me none. But it makes Jesse shaky. Confused. Thinks he's stupid."

"I can't help it if Mother is a school teacher and taught me those things. Besides, not knowing how to read or write doesn't mean you're stupid. Just means you never had any schooling."

She shrugged. "Don't tell Jesse I told you. He'd be powerful mad if he knew."

Wonderful. Another secret.

"You gave him a black eye."

Satisfaction swelled his chest.

"Quit grinning like a possum. You don't look so good neither. Got a busted lip. Gonna swell up bigger than a toad."

He touched his upper lip and flinched. "He hits hard. Feels like one of his beloved horses kicked-in the side of my face."

Flicking ashes from the cigarette, she nodded and cleared her throat. "Speaking of horses, that sorrel of yours is a beaut. Runs like a deer."

"Thanks. Tom's pa said the exact same thing." He didn't mean to go on but liquor had a hold of his tongue. "Red was a gift. From Mother. Didn't want me walking." Melancholy crept into his words. "She traded her wedding ring for him. She tried to keep it a secret, but I knew." His voice cracked. "That gold band was the only thing she had left of Father's."

"Damn."

Her swear broke his reverie. "What?"

"You mean to tell me your ma did something like that just so you wouldn't have to walk?"

The question touched a nerve. Unwanted tears filled his eyes. Crying, like a kid. Sure didn't want her to see. He ducked his head and took another swig. "Thought I'd be safer on horseback, I guess. Just wanted to protect me. That's what mothers do."

"Not mine."

He watched her jab the smoldering butt into the ground. "You mean your ma doesn't care about you?"

"Hell no. Bet ya a month's blue-backs she never wants to see me or Jesse again."

Surprised at the bitterness in her voice, Charlie wrestled with the notion of a mother not loving her child. The thought never occurred to him. Lord, he took Mother for granted.

"I ain't got no body what loves me like that. Not a ma. A pa. Beau or husband."

Her candid admission tugged at him and in a flash of insight, he understood her. She wore a mask of arrogance and defiance to protect herself from loneliness and hurt. She just wanted what every person wants, love. Her innocence and honesty grabbed his heart and the aching need to comfort her surprised him. He fumbled for the right words.

"Jess does."

A slight smile tugged her bee-stung lips, but sadness edged her words. "I know. Ain't the same, tho'."

An awkward silence settled around them. The bubbling creek sounded too loud and out-of-place. She stood and walked to the water's edge. The moon's yellow eye peeked over the horizon. He followed and waited for her to talk first.

"I think falling in love would be the best feeling in the world, don't you?" She turned to face him. A slight blush painted her cheeks a dusty rose. "I mean, having someone to stand by you no matter what ya done wrong and still love ya for who you are would be such a comfort."

Her words swept him to the past and Mother whispered in his ear. "*Never forget. No matter where you go. What you do or become, I will always love you."* Not having someone to care would be worse than any battle ever fought. Jess and Emmie only had one another. Like a fool he'd threatened to sever the thread that held them together. No wonder Jess hit him.

An overwhelming urge to console her made him reach out without thinking. Lifting her chin with the tip of his fingers, he stared into eyes wet with unborn tears and saw the true Emmie. Shy. Compassionate. Vulnerable. The stain of pink in her cheeks brought out a sweetness in her face. Butterflies fluttered in his stomach. His voice, soft and hushed, whispered. "Never wanted to hurt you. Not sure neither you nor Jess could survive without the other. But I made a mistake. I had no business making that decision. It was wrong of me."

"I know."

And just like that, the mask was back in place.

She turned to leave, then stopped. "You gotta do what you think is right. That's just what men do."

Shocked, he stammered, "What…what did you say?"

"That's just what men do." She cocked her head to the side and studied him. "Why?"

He took a deep breath. "Do you…do you think I'm a man?"

"Funny question."

Shouldn't have said that. Time for him to bare his soul. "It's just…just…well, I don't feel like one. Most of the time I think I'm just a clumsy kid."

She walked back to him, chewing her lower lip. A trait she shared with her brother. "That what you were talkin' about when you told Jesse you had something to prove to yourself?"

The tip of his boot kicked at the rocky creek bank.

He ducked his head. "You think I'm stupid, don't you?"

"Yeah."

The softness of her voice contradicted the callousness of her words. He gazed up at her. She took a step toward him.

"I've never told anyone that before, except Mother. Don't know why I confessed it to you. Must be the whiskey talking."

She smiled. "Don't you know? Moonlight pulls secrets out of ya.' Want to know what I think?" Her blue eyes reached out and tied him to her.

"Guess so."

"I think you're so busy worrying about being a man that you lost sight of the fact that you are one. Maybe you were a boy when you left home, but you're all man now."

Simple words that broke the heavy yoke of self-doubt he'd carried for so long and made it fall from his shoulders.

"Emmie. I won't tell. About you being a girl. Your secret is safe with me."

Another step closer.

"Told ya, ain't no girl. Became a woman the day I made up my mind to take my life into my own hands."

She pulled him to her and kissed him. Full on the mouth.

"And I don't kiss boys."

With a springy bounce she was gone, disappearing into the mist and mystery of dark night like a blithe spirit. What just happened? Did he dream the whole thing? Every nerve in his body danced like he'd been hit by a lightning bolt.

Dizzy, he slumped against the cool bark of the

nearest sycamore tree and slid to the ground. He touched his lips still moist from her kiss. Oh God! Hope he didn't slobber all over her like a love-sick calf. And his breath! Smelled like whiskey. Huh. How amazing. His busted lip didn't hurt anymore. And her lips, so soft and cool. Why'd she do that?

Wonder if she liked the kiss as much as he did? Next time would be better. Oh Lord, would there be a next time? He grinned. Oh, yeah. Only next time he'd be ready. He'd kiss her first.

He tried to stand but his legs were shaking like a baby calf. Still weak, he slumped against the tree.

The kiss sent shivers up his spine but it wasn't the only thing that unnerved him.

Something strange happened when she touched him. A warm sensation overtook him.

The eerie scream of a screech owl dissolved the impression and brought him back to his senses.

He chuckled. *First taste of whiskey mixed with your first kiss too much for you to handle, Charlie boy?*

A deep sigh traveled from the soles of his feet to the top of his head. What a night. Magical and full of secrets. Red started the secrecy. The ring was next. Then Specks. Now Emmie. But the biggest confession of all warmed him to his core. Couldn't explain it. Knew it was fast. Didn't care.

He was a man, falling in love.

Chapter 35

Emmie licked her lips and smothered a giggle. Had to keep pretending to be a boy. Wouldn't look right to be caught giggling like a foolish Sunday-school girl. Yet it was hard not to.

Her mind flashed to Jenny Thompson. How jealous she had been of Jenny's looks. Golden hair, sleek and silky, that curled perfectly around her flawless face. Milk-white teeth that flashed in a cute, come-here-and-kiss-me kind of smile that made the boys act stupid and weak in the knees. Brown doe eyes with thick black lashes. Jenny was every plain Jane's nightmare. But Jenny only kissed boys. Gawky, mule-headed boys. A tiny laugh escaped. So much time wasted on nothin'. Today she had turned the tables on Jenny. She kissed a man. And he kissed back. Don't know what caused her to reach out and grab him like that. Wasn't planned. Just happened.

She flicked her tongue over her mouth to savor the last memories of his kiss. Never would have thought lips could be so tender. Eyes closed, she relived the moment. The sweet, musky scent of him. The heat of his flat chest warming hers. A hint of whiskey flavor on his lips and breath. And that look on his face when she pulled away! Confused, red-faced, and so good-looking her heart about busted.

"What's wrong with you?" Jesse asked. "Got a

dopey look on your face. Did you find Charlie?"

"Yes."

"Well? What happened? Is Mr. Know-it-All gonna spill his guts about us?"

"Don't call him that."

She sat next to him, ignored his stare, and gazed into the twigged campfire. "Everything's fine. He ain't gonna say nothin'."

"Gone a long time. What were ya doing?"

"Talkin'."

"About what?"

Her temper flared. "It don't matter. Our secret's safe, that's all that counts. He's sorry. Knowing him, he'll apologize."

"Knowing him? What's that supposed to mean?"

"Nothin'. I'm hungry. Let's eat."

Charlie's shadow loomed large on the ground. A tingle raced up her spine. She jumped to her feet. "Ah...ah...me and Jesse are goin' to get some grub. Wanna come?"

A shy smile spread across his face. A shiver tickled the back of her neck. *Dimples. He has dimples.*

"Sounds good."

He turned to Jesse and held out his hand. "Sorry for the misunderstanding." He pointed at the bruise under Jesse's eye. "Good shiner. No hard feelings?"

Jesse stood and took his hand. "Forget it," He chuckled. "You got a fat lip, there."

"Goes good with my thick head."

Emmie joined in their laughter. She hung back from them and watched Charlie walk toward camp. His stride slow and easy, like his voice. A deep sigh. How could she get closer to him without it looking strange?

Gotta be a way.

She lied. Wasn't hungry. Kept glancing out of the corner of her eye at Charlie. When he tossed another log on the campfire, he caught her stare. She ducked her head and pushed beans around on her plate. His slight chuckle made her smile.

After supper, guards were posted, and everyone settled in around the fire. Jesse nodded to her. "Come on, we sleep by the horses." She cast a look at Charlie. Didn't want to go. But it would look too funny if she didn't. Maybe he'd come check on Red and she'd get a chance to talk with him. She dogged Jesse's steps back to the picket line.

Jesse stoked the coals and added more kindling to the small campfire. She sat in the flame's orange glow and hugged her knees to her chest. Wasn't sleepy. Should be after the day she'd had, but her mind churned. Jesse stretched out on his back and stared at the star-lit sky. Horses snorted. A coyote yipped.

"Ever wonder what we're going to do after the war?"

His question caught her off guard. "Don't look like the fighting is ever gonna stop. Never thought about it."

"I have." Jesse flipped over on his stomach. "One day this thing will end. And I'm gonna miss it."

"What? Miss it? Can't believe you'd say—"

"Let me finish, Miss Priss. Ain't gonna miss the killing and fighting. But I like being part of somethin' as big as the Army. And takin' care of the horses. Makes me feel needed, like I got a purpose for being." He lowered his head and drew circles in the dust with his finger.

"Been feelin' lost for a long, long time. Think I

found a place where I fit. So, I've been figuring hard about what I want to do after this mess is over and done with."

"You mean, if we don't get killed first?"

He laughed, sat up, and folded his legs, Indian style.

She shook her head and shrugged. Okay, she'd play along. "So, what did you come up with?"

A deep breath. "Gonna stay in the cavalry. No matter which side wins. Go out West, fight Injuns, and take care of the general's horses."

Stunned and speechless she stared at him. Where did she fit in this plan? Didn't want to fight nothin', nowhere. Wanted young'uns, a home, family. Jack ass never once thought of her. The wind whistled through the big hole he'd shot in her heart.

Fighting tears, she leaped up and ran to the creek ignoring his calls to come back. First Pa left her, now Jesse. Would she be alone all her life?

A twig snapped and she tensed. "Go away! Got nothin' to say to you."

"What'd I do?"

She whirled at the deep voice.

Charlie stood staring at her.

"Thought you was Jesse."

He took a step toward her. "You crying?"

Oh, Lord. Must look a mess. She sniffed, turned her head, and swiped at the tears. His warmth came up behind her.

"What's wrong?"

Don't tell him.

Don't dare cry.

But she did.

"Jesse told me after the war, he's gonna stay in the Army. Go west and fight Indians." A ragged sigh. "What am I supposed to do?" She gazed up at him. "I can't go with him even if I wanted, which I don't. Tired of acting like a boy. 'Sides can't do that forever. Already poking out in places where a boy shouldn't."

"Oh, Emmie." His gentle laugh rippled through the warm night air. "Do you always say the first thing what comes to your mind?"

Blood pounded in her ears. Angry at herself for being so embarrassed, she snapped at him. "Well, pardon me for being who I am. If ya don't like it, then leave."

"But I do like it."

She stood there, blank, amazed, and shaken.

He walked to her and stopped inches from her face. Warm nutmeg eyes sprinkled with a pinch of moonlight never left hers for a moment.

Goosebumps popped on her arms.

He traced his fingertip across her lip.

Oh, God! He's gonna kiss me.

Slowly, ever-so-gently, he leaned in and touched her lips with his.

Knees buckled. Heart pounded. Light headed and giddy, she asked, "Like anythin' else?"

His smile deepened into soft laughter. "Your eyes, bluer than robin eggs." With a bold move he reached out and placed his hand over her heart. The heat from his palm seared his touch forever in her chest, like a brand. "Your soul, brave and bold." He dropped his hand and searched her face. Dark eyes caught and held her captive in their glow. "Your spirit, so wild, free, and passionate."

"What's passionate mean?"

A wide grin deepened his dimples. "Hot-blooded."

She giggled. "Kinda like the sound of that."

He laughed. "Perfect example."

She turned toward the water. The wind pushed dark clouds past the moon. A hint of rain trailed behind it. She shivered. "You said I was brave. I ain't. There's things what scare me."

"Like what?" He stepped to her side.

She wanted to tell him so bad, but could she open her heart to him? Would he laugh? She shot a quick peek at his face. Sincere. Honest. Handsome. Looking back at the shimmering, moon-struck water, she took a deep breath.

"Dying an old maid, never knowing the love of a good man or having young'uns."

He sank to the ground and sat crossed-legged. Reaching up, he took her hand and pulled her down to sit next to him.

"Isn't a chance in hell of that happening. You're too pretty. Got too much love in your soul for it not to reach out and capture a man's roaming heart."

Never in her life had she heard better words.

She squeezed his hand and leaned into him. Didn't want to talk anymore. Would ruin the moment.

He shifted, picked up a small pebble, and skipped it across the stream. "I want to spend more time with you." Looking at her face, he smiled. "Get to know you better."

She returned his smile. "Feel the same way."

"Been thinking on how we could do that without it looking strange. What with you being a boy and all."

She grinned. Funny how he thought the same way

as her. She laid her head on his shoulder. Felt his chuckle on her cheek.

"Come up with a plan. Every night after supper, we can sit together by the fire, and I'll teach you how to read and write. Won't look suspicious to anyone. Have to sit close to show you the books and paper."

"Damn good plan."

He squared around to face her. "Quit fretting about the future. Would bet money you'll find someone, have a family, and never be lonesome or alone again."

Her heart skipped a beat. He sounded so sure. Dare she believe? "Swear it."

His square jaw tightened. A serious look darkened his face and he crossed his heart.

"I promise with every ounce of my being."

Soft wind blew.

The full moon wrapped round them with golden arms.

Night creatures passed a gentle serenade back and forth to each other.

He sealed his vow with a kiss.

Chapter 36

"Saddle up, boys," Gumpy bawled. "Movin' out in thirty minutes."

Jesse stuffed belongings into his bedroll and glanced over at Emmie. "Wonder where we're heading?"

Her shoulders shrugged.

Tom overheard the question. "I really don't care. Just glad we finally got some orders and we're getting out of here. This place gets on my nerves. Hear that screech owl last night? Damn thing been caterwauling for two nights now."

"Spooks ya, don't it?" James teased. "Act like it's some kind of haint or something. Hell. It's just a bird."

"Don't tell Pa that." Tom rolled his eyes. "He hates the damn things. Claims when one starts to yell and holler death ain't far behind."

Charlie shivered. "Mother says the same thing."

"Y'all are acting like a bunch of scared rabbits," Jesse said and swung into the saddle.

He yelled at Gumpy. "Hey, Sarge! Where we goin'?"

"Arkansas."

Emmie rode up beside Charlie and squinted into the early morning sun. "How far is Arkansas?"

Jesse watched her rein in close to Charlie and Red, almost stirrup to stirrup. She'd been acting goofy ever since the fight. If he didn't know better, he'd swear Emmie was sweet on Charlie. He scoffed. Couldn't be true. Emmie never paid no mind to boys. But then again, Charlie weren't no boy. He'd rescued her from certain death. Girls like that in a man.

The lieutenant pulled his big dun up short and his voice boomed. "Men, our orders are to ride into Arkansas and meet up with General Thomas Hindman. He'll cross the Boston Mountains and join with us. Speed is crucial. We ride hard, only stopping to rest the horses. No hot food. Hard tack and jerky. No fires. We move out in ten."

He reined the dun around. "Brown! Need to see you."

Frosted fear gripped Jesse's heart. What could this be about? He shot Emmie a guarded look. Her face showed no emotion, but the biting of her lower lip betrayed her worry.

Jesse rode back to the lieutenant's tent and dismounted. Saluting sharply, he waited. Seconds stretched into eternity. The muscles in his forearm cramped. At last the lieutenant returned the salute and wasted little time in getting to the point.

"Brown. It's imperative we reach Arkansas quickly. I'm counting on you to keep our mounts in top notch condition. Check them regularly. Let me know straight away if there's a problem with any of them. That clear?"

Relief melted his tensed nerves. His and Emmie's secret was still safe. He snapped to attention. "Yes, sir."

"Good. Dismissed."

He turned on his heel and started back to his horse. The lieutenant's voice halted him in mid-stride.

"Brown, one more thing."

Again Jesse's heart slammed hard against his ribs. How long could he continue to play this game? Felt like a yo-yo on a string.

The lieutenant walked to within a few feet of him and stared hard. "Family is the most important thing in the world. I've noticed that your...brother sticks close to your side. I'm going to be honest with you. Don't like him being here. I wouldn't want either one of you to witness the death of the other." A sudden change in his tone made Jesse listen close.

"Your brother's spirit is admirable. There's a certain strain of independence and pride running through him. Learning to read and write, for example. Wants to better himself. I admire that. My little sister has a similar trait." He turned and walked away. Jesse struggled to hear his words. The man talked more to the wind than to him.

"I also know what it's like to protect one's family. When threatened, a certain instinct takes over. It's surprising what a man will do to keep his loved ones safe." He turned back to Jesse and his voice softened. "I know you will instinctively protect your brother first, and I should've sent him home outright. But horses are our life blood and take first priority. Don't make me regret my decision to let your brother stay. Understand?"

The lieutenant knew. Somehow he guessed Emmie was a girl. But for some unknown reason, he was letting the charade continue. Maybe Emmie reminded him of his younger sister. And what did he mean, "I know what it's like to protect one's family?" Jesse held his superior officer's stare without blinking and nodded.

"Yes, sir."

He'd never be able to prove it, but a faint smile crossed the lieutenant's face. Jesse saluted and mounted his horse. He owed the man.

He winked at Emmie and guided Patch up beside her. She gave him an anxious look. "He knows," Jesse said.

Fear bleached all color from her face. "What?!"

"Don't worry. He don't care. Hell if I know why. Just keep pretending like you have been and everything will be fine."

The lieutenant was right. They rode hard for days, only stopping for a few hours here and there to rest the horses. Jesse babied them and watched every stride they took like a hawk. Wasn't going to let the lieutenant down.

On a frosty morning in early December, they crossed the border into Arkansas. Worn to a frazzle, James and Tom grumbled and slumped in their saddles. The lieutenant halted the column. Lines etched his chiseled face and stubble dirtied his usual slick cheeks.

In a raspy voice he called out orders. "Make camp here. Plenty of hills surrounding us for protection. We're ahead of schedule. Rest up. We'll stay here a few days before moving on. Dismissed."

"Good," Tom said and swung to the ground. "Maybe we'll get some hot grub tonight. And coffee. Been so long since I had a steaming cup of coffee, forgot what it tasted like."

"You said a mouthful." James laughed. "I'm hungry as a bear. Don't know what I want first, food or sleep."

"Rub down and feed your horses before you do

either one," Jesse said.

Emmie noticed the looks James and Tom shot at Jesse behind his back.

"Why you being so hard on them? All of us know to take care of the horses before ourselves. We're tuckered out and cranky. If ya don't ease up, you'll have a fight on your hands."

"Quit tellin' me what to do, little Miss Know-it-All."

"What's the hell does that mean?"

Jesse tied the end of the picket line around the big maple tree and grunted. Fed up with her mooning over Charlie, his temper snapped, and he squared around to face her.

"What's goin' on with you and Charlie? You been in his hip pocket ever since the night of the fight."

White faced she gasped. "Someone say somethin' to you about it?"

Funny question. Why would she care, unless there was something going on other than schoolin.'

"No one's said nothing."

She slipped the snaffle bit from the Appaloosa's mouth and replaced it with the soft halter. The fresh scent of coffee drifted through the air, and she dodged his question. "Smells like Jumper heard Tom's wish. Be good to get some hot food." She glanced at him. "A full belly might make you feel better."

He stepped closer. "I feel fine. Just tired of you actin' so uppity. Never cared about reading and writing before. Why the sudden interest in it now?"

"What's it matter to you, anyway? Charlie would teach you, if'n you asked."

He finished tying off the other end of the line.

Behind him he heard the dull thud-thud of hoof beats. "I gotta help bed these horses down. Better run find Charlie, don't want to be late to class."

She stuck her tongue out at him and mumbled something under her breath about "hard-headed jack ass." If she wouldn't give him a straight answer, he knew who would. After supper he'd corner Charlie.

Jumper outdid himself. Hot beans, hushpuppies, cornbread, and sweet potatoes. Jesse piled his plate high then walked back to the picket line. Emmie sat by Charlie. Tom shoveled food in his mouth faster than he could swallow. He reared back and patted his belly. "Full as a tick. Wonder where that ol'geezer found sweet taters?"

Charlie stood, poured himself another cup of coffee, and grinned. "Probably the same place he hides that corn mash of his."

"Hey, Charlie," James said. "Jess needs to see ya. Down by the picket line."

Charlie cast a puzzled look at Emmie. She shrugged. He walked away from the fire and headed toward the horses. He found Jesse leaned back against a tree, smoking a cigarette.

"James said you're looking for me. Something wrong with Red?"

"He's fine. We need to talk."

Charlie eased down beside him. Gray smoke from the cigarette circled around his head then vanished in the cool night air. He sneezed.

Jesse took a long pull and looked him straight in the eye. "Need to know what's goin' on between you and Emmie."

Charlie met his gaze. "I'm teaching her to read."

"Sure that's all you're showen' her?"

Charlie's teeth clinched. "Don't want to tangle with you again, Jess. But I don't like the sound of that question."

"It's a fair one. She's my sister. Got a right to know what your intentions are."

"What did she tell you?"

"Nothing." A deep sigh. "Charlie, I ain't got no quarrel with you. Used to know every thought in Emmie's head. But no more. Danged if she ain't changed."

"In what way?"

He stubbed the smoldering cigarette against the tree bark and stood. Patch reached out his velvet nose and nuzzled his pocket, looking for a treat. The sound of Gumpy's harmonica drifted through the night air and soft laughter came from camp. "She's always spoke her mind to me, but never to others. Remember what she said to you about danglin' parts?"

"How could I forget?" Charlie laughed. "Never heard any girl say something that bold."

"That's what I mean. Guess she's been acting like a man so long, she's turning into one."

"She sure as thunder doesn't kiss like one."

Jesse whirled. "What?"

"Whoa!" Charlie threw his hands up. "Her idea, not mine."

Speechless, Jesse stared at Charlie then broke into a slow grin. "That sounds about like her."

Jesse shook his head and chuckled. "Truth be known, I'm proud of her. Ma beat her down lower than dirt, both with the strap and her tongue. Never thought she'd get the gumption to stand on her own two feet and amount to something. Can't tell you how many nights I beat myself up for leaving her to face Ma by herself. Turns out it's the best thing I could've done. She grew up. Knows her own mind and don't let anyone run roughshod over her. But I wonder if that ain't a curse. Might scare the men off."

"Not the real ones. I admire her fire and passion."

Time slowed. Patch pawed the ground and shook his mane. Horses shifted their weight and stamped hooves. Charlie stood, blew on his hands to warm them, then shoved them deep into his jacket pockets. "Earlier, you asked me what my intentions were. You're right, it was a fair question and deserves an answer."

He looked Jesse square in the face. "I like Emmie. A lot. In fact, pretty sure I'm falling in love. If I was home, I'd court her proper. But we're here. Home is just a dream. So, I'm wooing her the best way I can. That's why I'm teaching her to read and write. She isn't the only one learning something new."

"You serious? She's mule stubborn, wild as the wind. Never know what she'll do or say next. Quite a handful to break."

Charlie smiled. "She isn't a horse, Jess. Don't want to tame her, just guide her when she runs."

A far-away look came to Charlie's eyes. "I get this funny feeling in the pit of my stomach when I'm around her. Feel like I could conquer the world when she looks at me with those shining bluebonnet eyes of hers. They drill right into my soul. Couldn't lie to her even if I wanted. She knows who I am, my flaws, my fears, my dreams. It's like she's the other half of me. We complete each other."

"Huh?"

"Damn, it's chilly. Wished you'd built a fire." Charlie pulled his jacket collar up around his ears to block the frosty air.

"Didn't know we were going to talk so long or I would have. Answer the question, how are you good for one another?"

"Emmie's daring and fearless. I tend to hang back and over think things. Miss a lot of opportunities that way. She'll push me to do better, take chances. She's built a wall around her heart, and it's hard for her to trust. I intend to break down that barrier one brick at a time. Want to prove to her I'm in it for the long haul." He grinned. "That's what I aiming for, anyway."

"You gonna ask her to marry you, ain't ya?"

Charlie kicked the ground and avoided Jess' gaze. "Thinking hard about it."

He reached over and clapped Charlie on the shoulder. "I'd be proud to call you brother-in-law." His eyes narrowed. "But don't never hurt her, Charlie."

"Never would, on purpose." He cocked his head at Jess. "If I did ask her, do you think she'd say, yes?"

"Yep. But don't drag your feet too long."

"Why's that?"

Jesse grinned. "Knowing her, she'll beat you to the question."

Chapter 37

Charlie walked back to camp, surprised to find tents pitched by the fire. Emmie walked past him. "The lieutenant said we deserved a good night's sleep and to set up tents to protect us from the frost. I know Jesse won't leave the horses, so I'm taking our tent down to the picket line." A forlorn smile pulled her lips. "It's late. Guess we won't read tonight."

He glanced around to see if they were alone. Big John sat drinking coffee by the fire. Damn. "That's okay, kid. We'll hit it a good lick tomorrow night."

She lingered for a moment, gave a surrendering sigh, and walked away.

He kicked the dirt in frustration. Couldn't wait for this damn war to end so they wouldn't have to sneak around and pretend.

"Night, Charlie," Big John said and lumbered to his tent.

"Yeah. Night."

Grumpy and not tired, Charlie poured a cup of coffee and slumped down beside the fire. A hint of vanilla drifted on the night air. Lieutenant must've lit his pipe. A deep breath. He could almost taste the smooth spice on his tongue. Maybe he should try a pipe. Might relax him.

A shooting star streaked across the inky heavens. Moonlight danced from tree top to tree top playfully throwing opalescent beams through the maze of branches and leaves. Not to be outdone, the night sky presented its blanket of glittering diamond points, spreading it from horizon to horizon. The Little Dipper mischievously skipped past his bigger brother and took his spot in the brilliant panorama of celestial light.

Flames licked at the wood. Hypnotized, he watched logs burn and twist into different forms and shapes. A snake here. A dragon there. Frayed nerves calmed, and his mind wandered.

What a strange game Life played. Here he was caught in the middle of hatred so evil that it threatened to destroy everything he knew; the land families, a race of people, even a whole nation ironically built upon the premise that all men were created equal. Yet despite the brutally and violence, he'd witnessed great love. His unit, for example. A hodgepodge of men different as night and day, bonded together like brothers under the watchful eye of a lieutenant older than his years. All grieved when one failed to return to the nest, and all celebrated when one did.

Then there was the love Jess had for the horses. He believed with all of his heart that it was his responsibility to protect and defend the innocent animals that they depended on so desperately. A duty he performed with both passion and compassion.

Who could deny the brother/sister bond that ran so deep a young girl willingly sacrificed her very identity to keep it intact?

Emmie. Spirited, shy. Emmie. So desperate for any kind of love. Who would've guessed out of all this hate the love she sought would be found, in him?

Mother. How could he forget her? She loved him

so deeply, that she sacrificed the only thing she valued dearly in order to keep him safe.

Coffee cup empty, he breathed a deep sigh. Life could be cruel, violent, and terrifying, yet Love was the great equalizer, the medicine that healed all. No matter how many times Love got beat into the dirt, the emotion always found a way to grow back. Thank God.

Fatigue finally took its toll, and he shuffled to his tent, careful not to wake James and Tom when he crawled under the blankets. Sleep pulled at his eyelids.

Wonder if the time would ever come when man would realize that Love, not money and greed, was the greatest power on earth? Maybe not in his lifetime. But he'd like to think so eventually, because, after all just like its cousin, Love; Hope is everlasting.

Wrapped in the comfort of that thought, he fell into a deep sleep.

Early morning fog hung heavy like a silver, smoky tapestry just above the tree tops.

Icy frost covered the underbrush and cast an eerie mid-evil spell on the land. The enemy mysteriously materialized from the heart of the woods. Phantoms of death floated swiftly through the mist. Violent. Murdering.

Charlie opened his mouth to shout a warning, but he never heard the words. Everything moved in slow motion. The lieutenant fell to the ground, his shaving razor clutched in his hand shaving cream on his face. Bullets riddled his back. He never knew what hit him.

Buried beneath pots and pans, Jumper looked up with sightless eyes. Charlie sobbed. Fate played a cruel hand. Jumper suffered the brutality of barbaric surgery losing not only a leg but his dignity as well. Yet he overcame his handicap with the determination and tenaciousness of a bulldog, only to be ambushed and cut down while making morning coffee.

He wasn't the only one that witnessed Jumper's slaughter. Gumpy, armed with only a sword, charged like a rabid animal, hacking away at the merciless blue-coated plague. His swinging blade cut only air. In a halo of gunfire, he fell and died only inches away from his boyhood buddy.

Tears streaked down Charlie's face.

Tom and James woke to gunfire and struggled to shake off sleep's paralyzing grip. The enemy stormed their tent and showered them with bullets. They never had a chance.

Charlie knew death called his name.

Emmie! Had to save her! And Red.

He ran in a zigzag pattern to the picket line. Pulling the slip knots along the line, he set the horses free. Red stood last. Tears mixed with sweat ran into Charlie's eyes. He swiped at them with one hand and pulled Red's halter off with the other. "Run! he cried.

Where was Emmie?

Jess tore past him, heading for the creek. Death ran beside him. Charlie saw blood running down Jess's leg, arms, and back, yet still he ran, refusing to acknowledge the life draining from his wounds. Charlie chased after him, and topped the hill a few steps behind Jess.

Emmie lay in a pool of blood.

He watched in horror as Jess struggled to lift her lifeless body into his arms. He faltered. Sinking to the ground, he turned to Charlie. His mouth opened, but no words came. Life left him and he slumped over Emmie, protecting her even in death. His promise fulfilled.

Charlie fell to his knees. God! All of them were going to die. It wasn't fair. To die in battle was one thing, but to be slaughtered…the Minie ball hit him between the eyes. Instinctively his hands flew to the spot. Only one word was on his lips, "Mother."

Hundreds of miles away Clara crumbled to the ground.

Chapter 38

"Over yonder, I plan on planting corn and in the next field, think I'll try my hand with potatoes and onions."

Clara stood in the middle of the unplowed field and shaded her eyes with a liver-spotted hand. Beside her, Specks talked about the crops. It was a game they played every year. They'd walk the fields together, and he'd ask her about what he should plant and where. She never answered, only nodded at his suggestions. Crops and farm work was his passion, not hers, but she loved him for including her in the process.

She turned and studied him. Four years of three-square-meals-a-day had filled out his lanky frame, and knowing he had somewhere to hang his hat, settled his scattered, often erratic behavior.

"Think tomatoes will grow good by that patch of dirt next to the house."

A slight smile was the answer he was looking for, and he continued to walk and talk more to himself than to her.

Four years? Had it been that long? Seemed like only yesterday she had taken him under her wing. The first few months hadn't been easy for either one of them. Skittish and awkward as a new-born colt, he tried hard to do everything perfect only to think harsh of himself when he failed. She struggled to walk the fine line between giving him encouragement and doing everything for him. Wasn't going to smother and lose him like she had Charlie.

Charlie. Dear Charlie.

No surprise Specks took to farming like a duck takes to water. The place never looked so good. He'd traded the oxen to Harvey Carpenter for a milk cow, chickens, a goat, some pigs, and a mule named Zeke, not Elmer. Mended the barn, fixed the fences, and even put a pump in the house. No more hauling water in the rain and cold. Who would have thought?

Schooling had been the turning point in their relationship. Every night after chores were done, they sat at the kitchen table with tablet and pencil. Sums, reading, and writing. Specks couldn't get enough. He had a quick mind and a hunger for knowledge. The time spent at the old wood table became they're favorite time of day, and the bond between them grew from mutual respect into love. The first time he'd called her Mama Ely, she cried for days.

Specks was heaven sent.

A tear slid down her cheek. Specks was her child even if her blood didn't run in his veins, but as much as she loved him, the hole in her heart would never heal complete.

Charlie's face flashed before her. She turned to the west. Tall and straight, her gaze never left the horizon. She'd heard his cry that day…that awful black day. Heard her only son, her baby call to her with his last breath. And she couldn't run to him. Save him. A mother's worst nightmare.

"Mama Ely? You all right?"

No answer.

Specks sighed, sat on his heels, and waited. Knew better than to talk to her until she shook free from the trance. Wonder what she saw this time? Should be used to her visions after all these years, but they still left him shaky and uneasy.

Downright spooky how many of her sightings turned out right, even if they were just small things; when it was going to rain, knowing what he was going to say before he said it, warning him about the rattler coiled on the other side of the log before he's stepped over it. He shivered. That snake was a granddaddy. Six feet long with a head bigger than a bucket. Stunk to high heaven. Damn thing would've swallowed him and his boots if she hadn't yelled at him to stop.

A quick glance at her. Still no movement. He shook his head. Never would understand what she called *The Shine*, but he'd never tell her so. Loved her too much.

He scooped up a handful of dark soil and took a long deep whiff. How he loved the smell of rich dirt and watching things grow. Turned out to be a damn good farmer. Who would've thought? Only Clara. She believed in him from the very start.

At first he felt shy and uneasy around her, but that changed when she taught him to read and write. Said no son of hers would go uneducated. Son. His heart about bust with pride. It was just as Charlie had said, Clara became his second mother.

The dirt slipped through his fingers. Charlie. Would never see him again. Or Jess.

A shadow passed between him and the sun. Clara reached for his shoulder to steady herself, and eased down beside him, tucking her skirt under her. Always took a few minutes before she told him what she'd seen. He waited, gazed out across the brown earth, and thought about how blessed he was to live with Clara and in the holler.

Cougar Hollow was charmed.

The first Sunday he'd gone to church with Clara, Preacher McGuire gave a sermon on brotherly love. Said it was only fittin' because of the war. Reverend McGuire talked in a soft voice so unlike the ranting and raving of Preacher Harris back home that he actually enjoyed and listened to the service. That Sunday, Preacher McGuire stood in front of his parishioners and declared that love was the one thing that could defeat hate and violence, so from that day forward, he would find something to love every day. He dared the congregation to do the same.

"Doesn't have to be big things," he said. "Love the sun for its warmth, the flowers for their beauty, the creek for the water, neighbors for friendship. Let joy and happiness fill your heart and keep hate at bay."

To his amazement, everyone accepted the challenge. The result? Peace. The war never touched the holler. Such a simple thing to do, yet it had worked…like a charm.

"Specks?"

His heart leaped at the sound of her words.

"The war's over."

Chapter 39

It took several months before official notification of Charlie's death reached them. An ambush at dawn, not some calculated battle. All members of Unit 547 buried in a mass grave somewhere in the Ozark hills.

The words hit Specks hard. Deep in his heart, he'd always hoped Mama Ely had been wrong. That Charlie and Jesse still lived.

Clara threw the notice in the fire. Watched the paper smoke and curl. Not one tear fell.

"The Good Book says, "For every time there is a season. Time for grieving is over."

Brave words from a brave woman.

She lied.

He heard her sobs in the still of night. Caught her holding Charlie's primer book, tracing his name printed in little boy scrawl on the inside cover over-and-over as if conjuring his memory back to her. The sight liked to ripped his heart in half. But he never spoke of it.

The storm changed everything.

Lightning forked the black sky. Thunder cracked whip-sharp and shook the small cabin. What was it about rainy nights that often birthed more sadness than one could shoulder? Clara sat in her rocking chair, knitting. He could tell by her far-away expression thoughts rested on Charlie, not the yarn or the clicking needles. Silence pressed his chest until he thought he'd bust wide open.

"Mama Ely? I can't bear seeing you so unhappy. Just know if'n you have a need to talk it all out, I'm here."

A slight nod of her head was her only answer. Almost ready to give up and turn in for the night he started toward his room. She stopped his footsteps with a deep sigh.

"I was thinking on something Alice said the other day. She mentioned how much easier it would be coming to terms with never hearing James's voice or laugh again if there was only something…anything of his to hold onto. We haven't any notion where our boys are. There are no names etched forever in stone. No graves to whisper a prayer over or leave flowers on." Her gaze lifted to capture his.

"Do you understand what I'm saying? After we die no one will ever know Charlie even lived."

He swallowed the lump crawling up his throat.

"That's as bad as sin, ain't it?"

"Don't say ain't, Specks."

He couldn't help but smile. Always the school teacher.

"Specks, I know Charlie loved me. Without doubt. But what really gnaws at me is that he died without knowing how much I loved him. Never told him the day he was born how my heart filled to overflowing. Never said how much joy and happiness he brought into my life. He was so young." She jabbed the knitting needles hard into the balled yarn.

"A mother should never outlive her child. Never. It's worse than any hell ever conceived."

This was the reason for her unyielding sadness.

"He knew, Mama Ely."

"How can you be so sure?"

The lump jumped into his gullet. He struggled to keep his voice from cracking.

"Because of this."

He crossed the room and kneeled by the rocker. With shaky fingers he fished the wedding band from the deep creases of his pocket and placed it in her hands.

"I'm mighty sorry, Mama Ely. I got the ring from Harvey Carpenter the first day I came to Cougar Hollow. I should've given it to you that day. I promised Charlie I would, but it was never mine to give back. I figured I'd just take good care of it until Charlie came home. Then when we found out he was dea...gone, I couldn't find the right time. Until now."

Her gasp filled the room.

"He knew what you did for him. How you traded the ring for Red." A deep breath. "He told me once the day he rode away from you was the worst day of his life. Never doubt he knew and carried your love in his heart. It's what made him the best man I ever knowed."

"Oh Specks."

Her words came hushed, almost reverent. Took every bit of gumption stored in his being not to break down and sob with her.

In hopes of lifting her mood he chuckled. "Red. Charlie loved every hair on that gelding's ears, neck, withers, and rump. Funny thing is, I think Red knew and loved Charlie just as much."

A smile broke through her tears. "I told Harvey to find me a winged Pegasus. Red was the first one he could catch."

"Can't help but think how much better this world would be if'n everyone would love one another as much as those two did."

"No truer words, Specks. No truer words."

Chapter 40

Heavy rain stripped away the dinge that had covered the valley. Specks stepped through the cabin door into air thick with the fresh scent of rich, moist soil and green grass. He could taste the sweetness on the tip of his tongue. Mama Ely, clothes pins clamped between her teeth, was busy hanging wash on the line. The storm chased away her gloom as well. Breakfast had been happy and comfortable, free of the cloud that dogged them for weeks. He'd laid awake most of the night thinking of some way to ease her pain. He'd finally come up with a plan. He crossed the yard to tell her. She turned.

"Specks? What is that? Over yonder?"

His gaze followed her pointing finger.

"Huh. Looks like a horse."

His breath froze. No. Couldn't be.

"Mama Ely. I think…it's Red!"

He felt her hand grip his shoulder. "Are ya certain?"

"Sure as shootin'. Oh, he's rail-thin and tarnished a mite, but I'd know that white snip and muzzle anywhere."

Her hand tightened. "Well, for land sake's stop gawking and go get him. I'll fetch a bucket of water. Be gentle. Poor dear looks plumb tuckered out."

No need to tell him twice. Specks broke into a trot,

then into a full-out run. If there had been any doubt the rusted sorrel wasn't Red it disappeared with the horse's low whinny. He'd thought he cried every tear stored up in him. But he was wrong. Fresh ones rained down his cheeks at the sight of the proud horse limping toward him. He buried his face in Red's matted mane and sobbed so hard he didn't hear Clara come up behind him.

"Oh, my poor baby. Everything will be all right."

"I know, but…" He choked back a chuckle. Her words of comfort were aimed at Red, not him.

"Oh my. He looks bad, Specks. Reckon' how far he's come?"

"Can't say. Don't know how far hell is from here. But don't fret none. He just needs some good oats in his belly and tons of loving care. We got plenty of both. Won't be no time at all till he's fit as a fiddle and as grand as ever. Let's get him home."

She fussed over Red all day. Even cooked up a warm mash of oats, molasses, and God only knew what else. He bit his tongue and gently scolded. "Don't give him too much at first, Mama Ely. Gotta ease him back into eating regular."

Course he had no business pointing fingers. He hovered over Red just as much. Heated water to scrub the grime from his coat. Brushed the tangles from the horse's mane and tail. Soothed and coddled way into the evening. Satisfied Red was comfortable, he lit a lantern, leaned back against the hay bales, and watched while the horse dozed in the glow. Mama Ely walked in, a blanket under her arm.

"If you're going to sleep out here with him tonight, you'll need this."

He laughed at her tease. She eased down beside him and spread the quilt over their legs.

"Mama Ely? I think Charlie sent Red back to us as a message of hope."

"So do I. With all my heart."

"I've been studying on what you said last night. About not having a marker with Charlie's name on it to visit now and again. Why can't we have one made and put right here? On the farm?" He turned to her. "He was born and raised here. Worked the land. Walked the fields. Just 'cause his body is gone don't mean his spirit is too."

She said nothing. Just stared. Damn fool notion. Should've kept his mouth shut.

"What would it say? The stone? What words should we chisel on it?"

"How about: Charles Ely. A man of truth and love."

She cleared her throat. "I think that's a right fine idea, Specks. Yes, sir. Mighty fine."

Her gaze swept the barn, passed him, and landed on Red. She reached for Specks' hand and squeezed. The gold of her wedding band reflected the lantern's soft light and danced on the wood walls.

"I like the words too. They be more than fitting." A gentle smile smoothed her wrinkles and she sighed.

"Because, after all, when all is said and done the only thing what matters is Love."

Epilogue

The Final Whispering

The book is finished!
The fourth promise is fulfilled.
Eureka Springs, Arkansas is a magical little town that I escape to when I need a mini-vacation. Most of the hotels are haunted. The Crescent Hotel is nationally known for the spirits who reside there. What better place to stay when intimate with ghosts?

To celebrate I take my niece and a close friend to Eureka for a weekend at the Crescent Hotel. Unknown to me at the time, Charlie tagged along.

"I feel good about the book," I tell my niece. "I wrote Charlie's story. Gave his words to the world to read. He's free at last. Now he can cross."

The three of us sit outside on the balcony at The Crescent and enjoy the folk singer performing that night. We bring our own bottles of beer to the small table, not knowing we are breaking any rules. The night turns cool. My niece and friend decide to return to our room for their jackets. I sit at the table, alone, and wait for them.

The waiter comes over and informs me that we will have to buy our drinks from the lounge.

"No problem," I say.

He clears the table and wipes it clean.

"Sorry, guys," I say to my niece and friend when they return. "The waiter took our beer away. If we want to continue to sit here, we have to buy from the bar."

My niece points at the table. "Well, whose drink is that?"

In stunned silence I stare at the glass sitting beside me. Only a split second passes, but it feels like an hour before I find my voice and say, "I have no idea."

"Are you sure the waiter took all the bottles away?" my friend asks.

"Positive. I've been here the whole time. I swear nothing was on the table."

The three of us circle the drink and study it as if it was a science experiment. The ice in the glass is melting, like it had been sitting there for a while. Finally, I snap. I pick up the glass and take a sip. My niece about wets her pants.

"I can't believe you did that. You have no idea what that is or where it came from."

"It's bourbon and branch water," I say.

"Branch water? What's that?"

It's what Southern gentlemen drank with their bourbon," my friend says.

Her statement hits home. The drink is from Charlie.

I take another sip.

"None of us like bourbon. Are you really going to drink that?"

I look at my niece and grin. "You're damn right I am. Charlie sent this drink to me through dimensions of time to express his gratitude and joy over the book. I wouldn't dream of not accepting it."

I raise my glass to the cool, misty night and smile.

"Rest in peace, Charlie. Cheers!"

~R. H. Burkett

A word about the author...

R. H. Burkett is a public speaker, Tarot card reader, contest judge, and an award-winning author with short stories in several anthologies, a list of contest wins, and her three published novels. She is a member of several writing associations and serves on the Board of Directors for the Ozark Writers League in Branson, Missouri. She currently resides in Springdale, Arkansas.

truthsbyruth.wordpress.com
rhburkett.com